DON'T
ASK
ABOUT
THEM

UNOS & OTROS

EDICIONES

A CIP catalogue record for this book is avaible from The Law Library of Congress of the United States.
Translation: Cesar Salazar

ISBN 10: 0998822299
ISBN-13: 978-0998822297

www.unosotrosculturalproject.com
felixfojo@gmail.com
www. felixfojo.com
infoeditorialunosotros@gmail.com
Made in USA, 2017
2da Editión

DON'T ASK

ABOUT THEM

Félix J. Fojo

How are you going to recognize the characters of this story, which is nothing more than a novel, if flesh and blood people don't even know themselves very well, that's why I tell you don't ask about them.

The author

To those who have to start all over again

Deceive the heavens to cross the ocean (Mán tián guó hái)

Book of Qi (Anónimo) (Aproximadamente siglos IV y III ANE)

Time is a triad: the present as we experience it, the past as present memory and the future as a present expectation.

Saint Augustine of Hippo (354-430 NE)

1

HAVANA, 1959

The man in the black beret explained to him, with the paused and slowed voice of a teacher, while they enjoyed a pair of stout and pestilent handmade cigars, that killing —executing sounded best, he clarified— was, in the long run, and inexcusable requirement of survival and a duty that history would reward with the eternal gratitude of the masses. In short, a revolutionary task.

"The dead, pibe, generally don't obstruct the tasks of the living, they don't argue, they don't fuck around", he said. "But above all they teach wayward people that making mistakes has its price".

"Everything does", said the clean shaved captain with his half-cubanized southwestern gringo accent that seemed funny to the one in the black beret.

"Yes, Herman, but for the deceased to be really useful to the cause, to the cause of us revolutionaries, they have to be many and their crimes well known". —He sucked in air, making a strange noise within his asthmatic chest—. "That is the importance of summary trials with prosecutors, a defense, journalists, photographs and television reminders, for the people to get in their thick heads that to defend them, that pleading for their mercy is to be an accomplice in their crimes". —He sucked in the smoke wrinkling his nose as if the blue vapor were a medicine—. "And with appeals, even if they're this fast". —He snapped the thumb and middle fingers of his left hand.

Herman was falling asleep, or better yet, he was stunned.

"Yes, sí... sí". —He held back a yawn with an obvious effort.

"Batista didn't learn anything from you Yankees, who created the Nuremberg Trials and going around accusing the losers of being war criminals".

He coughed and spat, turning his head to one side, a dark spit that he brought out from the deepest part of his battered lungs.

"Batistians tortured and killed people and then denied it, or said that they died fighting against the police or the army". —He looked at the time on his wristwatch—. "They made heroes and martyrs, not examples. Understand what I'm saying, Herman?"

"A stupid man. So stupid, fuck!"

There was a distant noise: bars opening and closing, locks and latches, orders in mute, an isolated cry, ominous noises of an old colonial jailhouse at nightfall.

"It's us or them, Herman, and if we want to last, it'd better be them".

"Yes, sí, better them". —He kneaded the injured knee that hasn't scar over completely yet, perhaps because of the lack of a good medical treatment and rest.

The one in the black beret looked once more at the luminous sphere of the Swiss watch that El Jefe had given him, probably taken from the personal fortune of some jailed politician for being a thief or from some General of the previous fleeing government.

"Go to your thing, pibe, enough talk for today, in less than an hour those under your command will shoot the 9 o'clock 21-gun salute".

"Yes, Commander, I'm leaving".

"Have you had dinner yet?"

" A little bit". —He grinned reluctantly—. "I prefer to have a strong lunch".

"Do you have a loose stomach?" —He laughed sarcastically with his crooked mouth, much to his ironic and peculiar style.

The captain rested his hands on the unvarnished rough-hewn wooden bench and stood.

"I'm used to it I guess, I don't know, sir".

The murmurs continued, the muffled sounds, but now increased in that enormous penitentiary installation that came to life —an irony— just at nightfall.

"Bullshit, you're not an old hag, pibe!" —He made a more or less kind gesture with his hand that never ceased to be an order.

"Go, *chico*, go now".

The man in the black beret stayed contemplating the gringo, his eyes narrowing with visible interest, doubtful. He was almost a child grown by force and living an adventure that he himself had sought

12

and that it would make him, no doubt, a man or it would destroy him until it turned him to ashes. Anyways, life will have the last word.

Herman was walking now at a good pace, not looking back, feeling the impassive and hard look of the man in the black beret. He was limping slightly on his right leg, but he was quite agile. He was moving toward the block of galleys where hundreds of crowded interns waited. Waiting for whatever the events, the commanders or chance would have to give them, or even destiny, for those that believed in it.

Walking through the gloomy corridor, a kind of tunnel excavated with picks and sledgehammers in the living stone three hundred years ago or perhaps more by black slaves who erected that fortification into a massive elevation of cutting and humid limestone rocks, desolate and threatening, right in front of the mouth of the sheltered bag bay that was supposed to guard and protect from the attacks of pirates, corsairs, filibusters, the English, the Dutch, and other slags of the envious and aggressive outer world.

At the other side of the narrow mouth of the port entrance canal, the beautiful city, bright, open, clean and full of sun or stars. Car headlights and flashes of neon light, skyscrapers and the proud malecón, life, joy, beer, rum, music, dance, sex, and now speeches and work. Yes, work, and hope, and faith in something with no definition, or faith in one man, only one, who will know very soon to remain alone to rise in solitude to the heights, and also a lot of what people call the future, somewhat vague and blinding, like the ever-unreachable horizon in the deserts but of which you hold on to in the growing and overflowing tsunami. Something always better than the past and the present, after all, always ahead, in perpetual motion. That nice thing that they crushed at the end of their speeches and rallys: the bright future.

The man in the black beret now looked at the little square of dark sky that the huge surrounding walls allowed him to see. Huge walls stained with the rusty green of ivy growing from the wet junctions of the square stone blocks, upward toward the light, pointing towards a sky they would never reach.

He took in his cigar once more and thought that there, in that fucking citadel that the revolution had put in his way —and in his incorruptible hands—, everything was gloomy and ugly, depressing, even the shit of the traveling birds that upholstered the hard, chipped calcareous floor they walked on. As if hope had stayed on the other side of the massive gate, where the sun warmed and life seethed.

And it was true, dammit, from the immense gates in, darkness reigned.

But what did it matter if him and others like him, like the little American, would clear the way for the future. Like gods, or like the god in which he didn't believe in, or pretended he didn't believe in... Oh, of course, the god which he didn't feared!

Fuck those prissy little sluts, those priests eating little shits, those kids with their little bangs and their first communion little vests, fuck them.

Once more, with his sharp, sad eyes he followed the captain once more, while scratching his uncleaned scaly little wisps of beard. He followed him impertinently until the little captain disappeared around the corner of the passage.

A shrill order to attention was heard, then a different one, sharp, in a different voice and a sharper icy tone, if something like that was possible. Orders that came bouncing and bouncing in the echo of the always cold and dripping walls.

The man in the black beret couldn't help it —gladly, he was alone, with no indiscreet witnesses—, a shudder.

He dropped the cigar butt on the floor without bothering to turn to crush it and walked slowly, thoughtful, to his spartan office.

Alone. Alone and willingly steadfast in his struggle with life.

2

Havana, 1962

To the rushed marriage —*casorio* the old women named that ritual in Cuba— of Captain Herman Markis and Miss Ana María Santana Donremí —hastily decided a couple of days earlier in an outburst of insane passion in the dimness of a little hotel, those cheap and by the hour hotles that the habaneros called posadas— attended only four people.

Only four, no more. The bride and groom, a friend of his — a retired officer of the rebel army suddenly discharged for very obscure reasons who was now serving as a junior officer in a Ministry—,and Gretel, Ana María's sister, a steely and athletic sullen-faced teenager with a heart of gold, who promised herself not to abandon the bride at a time like that even if it meant more screams, tears, humiliations and conflicts for her.

Oh, and the notary, a bald potbellied bow-legged gentleman, a little grotesque but always smiling and kind, dressed in his blue-green militia uniform.

The five of them, a little dazed and crazy for it to end, fulfilled their respective parts in the swift ceremony. The judicial official accelerated the process *macheteando* the reading of the minutes, Herman said yes, Ana María did as well, they exchanged rings that had already belonged to them for a while, Gretel and Herman's friend signed without reading the paper that perfectly could have been a death certificate or an electricity bill and the couple kissed at the notary's request. When kissing, in the mouth, no tongue of course, they both blushed as if being caught, they shook hands and all went back to their personal affairs. Except the amanuensis, who after straightening the portrait of the Martyr that hung on the wall and filing all the papers of the marriage, he had to continue with the next one –that was his job and the man was an exemplary worker–, a nice old couple surrounded by a bustling court of neighbors, friends, children, grandchildren and great-grandchildren.

Gretel, already at the bus stop, hugged her sister in a tight, long embrace as if she would never see her again. Then she waved goodbye to the stunned Herman as she climbed up, more like pushed by an avalanche of people, to the bus that would take her back home to her mother and her dark life.

After the execution of their father, half a year before, which by pure chance it wasn't conducted by Captain Herman Markis —he was admitted at a Military Hospital to have a surgery performed in order to repair his battered knee—, the Santana Donremí family had begun the marshy and increasingly steep decline toward crumbling and disintegration.

The deceased —the executed people's enemy, the one in the black beret would rectify—, Rubino Santana, Ex-Lieutenant Colonel of the Army of the Republic, first in his class in the Cadets School of the Constitutional Armed Forces had opposed the dictatorship of Fulgencio Batista for ethical and moral reasons, not for being a revolutionary, which he wasn't and didn't have it in him. The somewhat illusory and quixotic opposition had cost him his rank of Staff Officer and a few months of relatively benign military prison in an island jail —it has been written and said that it is Treasure Island, but in time Fidel Castro would change its name to " "— nestled in a low gulf and murky waters to the south of the Havana province.

When Castro triumphed, Rubino had been perceived as a kind of hero of honor and integrity, an example of a military man with a proud career, oblivious to the shenanigans and crimes of previous governments. An old soldier to whom the triumphant revolution extended its youthful hands and that's why the former Lieutenant Colonel immediately regained his position in the New Army, not his rank though, for the new masters didn't recognize those stars in an organization where the Supreme Chief proclaimed himself Commander, with capital letter C.

Everything went well, more or less, until Rubino began to allow his discontent to be seen, to mutter or to conspire perhaps —again—, to try to save the lives of several of his comrades-in-arms, a commendable intention that, obviously, he couldn't reach.. And he might also had conspired to explore, with others as naive as him, how to stop the unstoppable tide somehow of pro-Soviet communism that was already present in all institutions, government agencies, industries, schools and in all corners of the country in those turbulent times of the Cold War.

Once more the indelible and transparent Rubino Santana put forth in all the acts and decisions of his life the fucking stupid ethic and moral reasons as his wife, Ana, had recriminated him during a bitter argument, whom had an infallible sense of smell to vent disasters —witch radar, Gretel said—, was desperate and terrified at what was imminent. This had happened just a couple of days before he was detained, never again returning home or to his family.

To make the story short, the former Lieutenant-Colonel was arrested without the slightest resistance and in his own office in the Command of the New Army, interrogated without much violence or enthusiasm —what for, if he denied nothing and accepted everything— for a few days, tried as another Batista «criminal» and summarily executed by a motley firing squad, five hours after the brief trial in the same fortress where Herman Markis carried out his macabre bureaucratic functions, just as he described them when he was in the mood of making jokes.

The wife and mother, Mrs. Ana Donremí, an elegant and a very good looking woman at the beginning of her forties, loved her abruptly deceased husband —until very recently, a vital man and in excellent physical form— with a quiet but powerful passion that always reflected in her happy face and in her firm, although tolerant, motherly manners, except, and that was a very important trait, that she felt in the nape of her neck a nearing misfortune, that thick shadow of misadventure, that black bird of misfortune that she could perceive behind her as an unexpected newcomer.

And so, it was that fateful day of judgment.

Almost no one believed that such a good, chivalrous man like Rubino Santana was to be executed. Some optimists hoped he'd been given perhaps twenty or thirty years of prison, but she, Ana Donremí, smelled death with her witch radar —Gretel never said it in front of her but she took it for granted— and alerted her daughters in time, from the very morning of their father's arrest, to get used to orphanhood.

The man in the black beret defined him very well:

"That stupid bourgeois is so, so, so good that he's better suited to be in heaven keeping company with our fellow St. Peter".

"They're going to kill him, as sure as I'm Ana Donremí!" —The wife said as she kissed the crossed fingers of her right hand—. Don't even think that these miserable bastards are going to let a man like Rubino Santana live! —No one had ever seen her shouting and upset—. Or haven't you noticed the bastards that are ruling over us?

And she was right, as always, when it was about misfortunes and disasters.

And, as expected, after this sudden fatality, of that sudden terror, Ana Donremí never was what she once had been. The unbridled hatred and with no boundaries to the system, to the government and to the sons of bitches who had left her a widow and orphaned her three children, killed her appetite to live, dried her soul and ate away her sanity and reason.

Day after day they had to almost shove her out of the cemetery, where an unmarked tomb, with a little wooden cross nailed to the dry ground and marked with a number and a letter on top in white chalk, lied Rubino's pierced corpse. There were doubts as of which of the dozens of tombs with those that were executed in that secluded, little-visited strip of this immense Havana cemetery was exactly that of her husband. For the day, the night, in fact, of his execution —an important word of the affair according to the man in the black beret—, he wasn't alone. All the alleged conspirators, except the informer, suffered the punishment early that morning, and the undertakers, who didn't care about that mess, were not particularly careful in the matter pertaining to the earthly order of those that weren't longer among us, especially if those bodies that had been shattered by six FAL rifles, thrown in unpolished wooden boxes, had in their lifetimes been enemies of the country and the revolution, a revolution that, moreover, paid their wages and gave schools to their children.

And, to entangle things even further, one disgrace wasn't enough because they never came alone, the eldest son of Rubino and Ana, Máximo Santana Donremí, twenty something years old, had fallen prisoner almost at the same time as his father, although in a different episode, and not by mistake or a big crime but for candor and being a big mouth, more of a *comemierda*, according to the same commissioners that throwed him behind bars.

Máximo, an engineering student at the *Universidad de La Habana*, was quick to join a counterrevolutionary organization, one of many that, as would be known many years later, had been created by the government itself to attract, like glue to flies, and to neutralize, the probable or dormant enemies of the classes. Enemies that swarmed and swarmed until the very day when the proletariat would finally and absolutely triumph, and then, and only then, would the new man be completely free and wouldn't need commissars, judges, jails or firing squads, but until then...

They condemned him —the declaration of two repentant conspirators was more than enough— in a summary process in which, inexplicably, between more than fifty people, was indicted only one capital sentence, one, which if not a record it was a good average. Máximo was sentenced to twenty years in prison, a bargain, and the boy began to fulfill the sentence just a month after his father's execution, and to make matters worse, in the same prison: that gloomy colonial fortress called La Cabaña

It was there, when visiting his brother to see him for two minutes and bring him a canvas bag with a pair of underpants, a toothbrush, some bars of guava candy, some gofio and a quarter of a liter of condensed milk repackaged in a plastic pot, where Ana María Santana Donremí, the eldest daughter of the late Rubino and Ana, met the Captain Herman Markis, while she was neatly searched by two militia women —a prerequisite before she could see and embrace her brother Máximo— under the watch of Herman who watched with a stern face and military gestures the strict compliance of the prison rules during the restricted schedule of family visits.

It was either love at first sight, or an overwhelming mutual attraction, or the still unknown endorphins, or a shared whim, but whatever it was, was. And how innocuous, obvious, even romantic —a word ridiculed by the new ideology— and beautiful, very beautiful.

And it was, of course, a cataclysm.

A superlative cataclysm.

3

Guanabo Beach, 1963

Ana Donremí, unexpectedly, got out one day from her somber amazement to make her position clear before the veiled insinuations of emigrating from the island.

She was unequivocal and unappealable: while her son was locked up in a prison and her husband in a pit of that country of vile savagery, she wouldn't move from there, whatever happened. They could all go into exile, to hell, wherever they pleased, but she would accompany to the end, like a shadow, like a soul in pain, the jailers and gravediggers who all the time prowled the two men of her life.

"Go away, fucking leave, and leave me alone with my ordeal!"

She slammed her fist into the wall and when she turned to go back to her room and her world of darkness reaffirmed in a hoarse voice that no one had heard before: "And no one even dare to mention such a thing!"

And she closed the door with a blow that knocked pictures and ornaments down several feet.

Little less was heard from her from that moment forward.

To visit Máximo every once in a while —the visits were spaced out more and more because of the prisoner's rebel position against an institutional way of bowing down to the authorities which they called reeducation— and sit in a canvas chair to watch over her husband's tomb and to chat with him in a very low voice almost every day, were the only known occupations of the widow, which ended in making her a common spectral figure for the employees and the occasional few visitors to the vast necropolis.

Only when a visit to her son was due, Ana Donremí unleashed a frenzied activity in the kitchen, preparing dishes and pots of tasty meals —obtained in the street with a thousand and one sweats and jolts by Gretel's ant-like work—, most of which would be seized, examined carefully, thrown away or devoured by the prison guards themselves, fed up with the everlasting white rice, kidney beans, and Russian canned meat given to them generously by the revolution.

The woman ate meagerly or didn't eat at all, slept very little at odds and ends, prayed in solitude or perhaps communicated with Rubino's spirit, who knows, sustained by the help of Gretel, a girl with the sullen look and heart of gold, the only person in that house with a small but relatively stable inflow of money, which was a very modest contribution, of course, given the lack of well-paid jobs for citizens so marked by the political situation of the island, or as was said in those times, not integrated into the revolutionary process.

Gretel, at eighteen, carried —without allowing to show anybody her bitterness and her fears— the world's burden, her shattered world, heavy as a huge bag of debris that had suddenly fallen on her back.

She studied math, English, chemistry, physics, calligraphy or whatever to kids in private schools that were still surviving in the environment, but now very close to being absorbed by the governmental educational system; she transcribed, with her good handwriting, documents and letters, nursed her children, in short, she worked through her life and that of her mother, and in a way and not in the magnitude she wanted, that of her imprisoned brother.

Some relatives and a few old friends, less and less, because they were leaving the island without pause, gave a hand, "lent" a few pesos, bought some small food bills for her and her mother or gave her used clothes but in good condition. All this was made with a lot of concealment, always keeping the distance to not be compromised.

The philosophical sentence —the guerrilla philosophy of the man with the black beret—: "the dead teach the living that making mistakes has its price", was demonstrating its functionality and effectiveness at a very fast pace, making friendship a crime and compassion a mockery. *Tirar una toalla*, that old Cuban rhetorical formula that explained why they gave a hand from time to time even to the most vicious rivals, was visibly out of date.

Ana María, the lady of Captain Markis, also collaborated, but in the most absolute secret. Only Gretel saw her from time to time, perhaps once or twice a month, in solitary parks and less busy cafes. The two women, like leaves in the wind, frightened, barely holding their will to hug and cry until they were dried up, both caught in the crossfire of repudiation brought to the extreme from Ana Donremí to her daughter: "The one that was my daughter and that I don't want to know anything about, nothing at all, the whore, the fucking whore that was able to lie down and wallow with the murderer of her father and her brother's jailer!"

And above all, Markis' growing difficulties in staying within the ranks of the army —the only home he had ever known in that little Caribbean island until the almost miraculous appearance of Ana María— after marrying the daughter and sister, all in one, of a pair of mortal enemies to the workers and the country.

Herman didn't even talk or see the man in the black beret anymore, now minister and all-powerful maker of definitive international speeches and radical economic policies. His guerrilla comrades had ascended to far superior positions, closed to him, or they had descended into prison hell, violent death or anonymity. And perhaps the worst: being an American had ceased to have popularity and the glamour of the early days to become a source of suspicion, as one young lieutenant of the militias had once told him, a helpful and highly disciplined mulatto who had mistaken him for a Russian instructor:

"As everyone knows, Comrade Captain, you Soviets are our brothers, unlike the gringos, who are all exploiting capitalists, racists and CIA agents".

He thought of explaining the truth to the boy but he preferred to keep quiet and let it go, why shake even more what was hopeless?

The beautiful rebel adventure, revolutionary, glorious and resplendent was over for Captain Herman Markis a long time ago. The youthful and solidary idea of helping to liberate a people from a dictator; to become, for that beautiful and smiling island, oppressed by a melodramatic General, into something like a Lafayette or a Pulaski, had turned into the creeping day to day of survival and suspicion. His adventurous and noble truth had served him to look with pride towards the future; his lies were now being more or less useful to hide his past and his true self, not with those above who knew him well, but with the subordinates, it was for the better that they didn't know him.

He no longer wielded his old bureaucratic role in that fortress of vampires —among which, he had perhaps unfortunately been the one with the longest fangs— and now he gave infantry training classes to recruits from all over the country who joined the new military service, and tried, if possible, to hide his true nationality, but common sense told him that this farce wasn't going to last long.

Moreover, his physical presence in that army that day by day was growing with officers formed in military schools of countries of Eastern Europe, began to be anachronistic, strange, almost improbable. He thought one day that he resembled an Indian with feathers, bow and arrows, with a horse without a saddle in a movie of Roman gladiators, and that wasn't going to last.

One afternoon, Herman met with Pardito, a tough, mischievous *guajiro* with whom he had shared the chill of the early morning hours and the hens —soups with feathers, they called them— that supposedly died of disease in the already distant times of the heroic guerrilla and tribal brotherhood of their brothers-in-arms, now he was a commander of the armored troops: Major Pardo.

Pardo, after shaking his hand with the firmness of a tanker, snapped at him without mincing words:

"American! *Chico*, are you still in these lands? You must have fallen in love like a madman of some female here, fucking hell! —And putting a big hand on his shoulder he let him now with one of those sly smiles that the Cuban peasants know how to give you advice without proving it—: "I thought you were up north, you boar, who can live there and you don't, it's true that God gives beards to those who don't have a jaw!"

That's why on a sunny Sunday with a light breeze he took his wife to the beach of Guanabo, on the outskirts of Havana, and while he caressed her tenderly, with the warm water of the Strait of Florida up to their chests and as far as possible from other human beings, he suddenly said:

"Ana María, listen to me, we're going to leave this place anyway we can, so that our children, those we are avoiding now, are born in a decent place".

She tried to look at him and the sun in front of her made her close her eyes, which increased the pair of fine tears that would come.

"I'll go, Herman, wherever you take me, wherever you want to go, anywhere. —There was not only resolution in her words but even an immense relief—. But what do we do, my love, with my sister and my mother?

From the warm and soft sand came the distant murmur of a battery radio with the twist, The Four Seasons, Elvis, The Beach Boys, Frankie Avalon, he couldn't tell. Cubans loved American music almost as much as theirs, and they used the beaches and a certain loneliness to listen to Floridian stations abolished and persecuted in the country.

Herman ran the fingers of both his hands over her face and almost burst out crying too, perhaps from relief that he had finally made that decision and a little impotence at what he knew to be inevitable.

"We take your sister with us".

Ana smiled with a vast and tired bitterness.

"Gretel will never leave, Herman". —She put her hands on his hard shoulders—. "She will never leave my mother and brother".

He was silent for a long second. Extremely long. He took a deep breath.

The music became more audible with a change of direction in the wind, it was the Zafiros, a very good Cuban group that imitated the Platters.

"You've heard of Commander Morgan".

She nodded with a sadness he had never seen before.

"I directed his execution". —He rinsed his mouth with sea water and spat—. "An American chosen to murder another American, and I did, do you understand?"

She nodded again, she pouted and pressed herself closer to him.

"For a sense of duty, out of fear, for being stupid, because my boss ordered me, for being an asshole, a coward, a fag, for whatever it was, there is no remedy for it Ana, and then, like a gunshot, you entered in my life".

She pressed her forehead against his, now he was crying.

"How long do you think it will take them to wipe me out? "

He hugged her tightly and as he always had, he felt that pleasant, quick erection that no other woman had provoked.

The music became dimmer now, far away.

Sweeter, even.

"Not only me, Ana María, wipe both of us out, to eliminate us so that there isn't even the memory of that". —He was whispering in her ear, though there was no one in more than fifty or sixty yards, only the soft, warm, relaxing movement of wind-curled waves.

"Both of us, Ana María, both of us".

He squeezed her until it hurt.

"I know, I always knew". —She superficially scratched his back with her fingernails.

"Removing us from the picture they'll make us invisible, as if we had never existed". —She gave him a flying, compulsive kiss—. "But if they need it one day, they will then say that the Americans killed each other, do you understand?"

She nodded, almost imperceptibly.

The music disappeared and the whisper of water remained as the only sound when the owner of the battery radio walked away through the sand.

"We've been here long enough, Ana".

"So, what will happen to them?"

"I'll see what I can do, Ana".

"Will you?"

"We'll see Ana, we'll see".

4

KEY WEST, 1963

"My name is Rafael, Captain Markis". —He let time float for a few seconds, as the manuals specified, but it came naturally to him—. "How did you manage to get here?"

"I think you know". —He said it without irony—. "We stole a motor boat between four former officers of the Cuban army". —He opened his hands frankly—. "We took it from a fishing cooperative that is in a place called Puerto Esperanza, a fishing village north of the province of Pinar del Río, as close as we could find to Florida".

Rafael, an unmistakable Cuban and obviously an officer of some US intelligence service seemed to nod.

"Actually, three former officers, Captain, you were still active".

"True, but I don't think I am anymore".

The Cuban ignored the comment.

"How did you come to an agreement? Taking into account the security control over there and the fear of possible betrayals".

Herman took his time to answer.

"I understand the doubts you may have, sir". —Herman knew perfectly well that he was talking to a professional.

"Forget my doubts, Captain, it's a question that falls out of the woods, doesn't it?"

"Everyone, the four of us, fought hard against Batista and we became friends in the times when friendship was valued, then things happened to us all, unpleasant things that disappointed us about that". —Herman shook his head in a slight denial—. "We came to the same conclusion by different paths, and once you get there, what else can you do?"

The Cuban, quite slowly, lit an unfiltered cigarette and offered one to Herman. He leaned forward and lit it with a cheap canary yellow lighter of the kind you buy in gas stations.

"Nice words, Captain, but they don't answer my questions".

"Either we trusted each other or it was all over". —He stared at the Cuban interrogator—. "I put forth the condition of taking our women with us, and in the case of one of them, divorced, his son". —He also leaned forward in his chair—. "If things got bad then we would all have died because it was clear that we wouldn't be unarmed, and when one has been in it when things turn ugly knows how to use *los hierros*, firearms, as they say in Cuba".

"I know, I know".

Rafael inhaled with satisfaction the spicy smoke of his cigarette and smiled as he let it escape through his nose wrapping himself in a brief white cloud.

He fumbled his hands to finish dispelling the smoke.

"It is a good explanation but it leaves out the whole process before the boat was stolen and the getaway, which, if one looks at it well, wasn't so difficult for four well-armed men in uniform, as you explain".

"Only one of us, former lieutenant Avilés, knew exactly of the place. —He nodded—. "Although I recognize that we all imagined it would be through there, since Avilés was the head of that cooperative, they called them 'delegates', of fishermen".

The Cuban threw the ashes of his cigarette to the floor with an indifferent gesture, though he looked around the ugly, uninhabited room for an ashtray he couldn't find.

"I don't doubt you, Captain, I also had something to do with the fight against Batista, but that's ancient history and it's besides the point". —He lifted a finger—. "But I want you to understand me". —His smile and his gestures were gentle, almost condescending—. "My job is to ask, and yes, it's true, sometimes to even doubt". —He stood up in slow movements—. "Four captains and lieutenants at once is something quite out of the ordinary, even for a country where there are so many bosses and where so many people want to leave".

Herman shrugged.

"I understand, sir, but we couldn't stop at those considerations when we were on the other side of the strait". —He smiled mischievously—. "Let's say, on the more difficult side".

28

The Cuban nodded and took a few steps through the small station of the Boca Chica military base, where they had been moved after an American coast guard rescued them a few miles from Dry Tortugas, west of Key West.

"How have you been treated?" —Maybe he was just making time, but there was warmth in his words.

"Very good".

"The ladies and the boy are well?"

"I think so, although I haven't seen my wife for several hours".

"She's well, Captain, and I can assure you that she hasn't been interrogated". —He lit a new cigarette and calmly exhaled the smoke—. And she won't be, at least for now.

"Thank you".

He seemed to brood for a minute, though to Herman it was obvious that whatever they were going to do it was already decided.

"Let's do something, Markis". —He used his surname with a little admonition, or maybe not, it was just Herman's paranoia working—. "We'll take you to a comfortable place in Miami where you can stay with your wives and get some rest from the trip".

"I think you're being ironic, sir, the trip wasn't even eighteen hours".

"Excuse me, Captain, I didn't mean to be ironic at all, I was thinking more of the tension of the previous days and, above all, I was thinking of those who aren't military". —He seemed sincere.

"As I said, we'll go to Miami and there'll be enough time to talk and think about the future, unless... —He looked at him quizzically—. "Unless you have some other idea in your head".

The Cuban took a seat again.

"No, no, sir, we are at your disposal".

The Cuban smirked.

"Good, better that way".

"My wife has no relatives in the United States, and mine..." —Herman looked at the floor—." I don't know where they are".

"You'll find them, if you look for them, of course". —Rafael scratched behind his left ear—. All in good time.

"Yeah, probably". —Captain Markis made a gesture of indifference, once more.

"Okay, deal then". —The interrogator rubbed his hands together as if they were wet—. "But for now, Markis, we will not leak anything of this desertion, almost en masse, to the press". —He put his index finger upright in front of his mouth in a gesture of silence—. "Discretion suits us all, at least right now".

"No *problema*". —Markis laughed at the way he said it—. "Our intention was to leave that behind, not making a fuzz of any kind, at least in my wife's and my case".

The Cuban laughed too.

"Markis, your case is a bit special, you're a citizen of the United States! Understand me?"

"Of course, I do, Mr. Rafael".

Rafael stood up.

"Come with me, Markis, enough talking, let's go and meet with your wife, don't you think?"

"Of course, sir, thank you".

"Then we'll see what your and our priorities are". —Rafael opened the door with courtesy but no affectation—. Maybe they match.

Herman went out into the hall followed closely by Rafael.

"Why wouldn't they, sir?"

They walked down a somewhat narrow corridor toward the exit.

"Come on, her peace of mind is what matters now".

"I'm truly grateful, sir". —Herman reassured him.

"No problem, Markis". —Both laughed at the occurrence— "Aren't we on the same side?

It was dusk".

5

Miami, 1963

From the point of view of easy orientation, its directions, the numbering of its streets, the monotony of the color of its buildings, Miami is an orderly city, at least more orderly than other less boring and vibrant cities.

If you look at it on a simple map, such as the ones you can get at any gas station, you will see that all the roads that go from north to south (or from south to north) are called avenues, and all that go from east to west (or vice versa) are called streets. There are exceptions and particularities but we won't complicate our life here over such insignificance.

Between avenues 122 and 137 and the streets 152 and 184, well to the south of the city, very close to the marshes and low zones, habitat of crocodiles and snakes that are the fauna characteristic of the inferior end of the Florida peninsula, there is a huge area with limited access, few buildings, which when viewed from the outside it gives the impression of being half empty and it also has a certain air of being a military settlement.

The former is false, it's true that grass and low shrubs abound, but what's said to be empty, it's not, and the latter is completely true, although in the blueprints it's indicated that these lands belong to the University of Miami, at least a good portion of it.

So, in the times of this history, inside, far from the curious glances of passers-by and a few neighbors, were, among other governmental units, the facilities of JM WAVE.

In 1963 —after the humiliating collapse of Bay of Pigs—; of the very dangerous bet of the Russian missile crisis in Cuba —which put, on those thirteen days of October '62, the lives of all the inhabitants of the planet on the edge of a razor; the stubborn implementation of the so-called Operation Mongoose, whose aim was to destabilize, and if possible to eliminate, the Castro government and Castro himself—, JM WAVE, that station of the Central Intelligence Agency had become a leviathan, one of the largest on the planet, and the most expensive. Its director, its head-honcho, Theodore «Ted» Shackley, known among his cohorts as Blond Ghost, perhaps because his hair was very blond and played old-school espionage from the heroic times of World War II —it was also said that they called him Ghost because he never let himself be photographed—, he was a complete monarch surrounded by his entourage and seconded by his vassals, many of whom had no idea of his existence, in fact, they didn't even knew for whom they worked for, or that in reality they received a salary from the CIA.

The "monarch" had his office in the so-called 25th building, a large house with a *Gone with the wind* style, a southern palace with columns on the porch, quite anachronistic for that time and that city with such a meager history.

Very few had access to that roomy, comfortable, airy but not an ostentatious place, from which Shackley, with his nautical charts, scaled maps, telephones and dictaphones, played to control the world, at least the Caribbean and Central American world that had been assigned to him by the Agency.

"Take a seat, Quintero, and tell me the news of your talks with the newly arrived Cuban officers".

There was empathy, a good communication between the two men, one, Shackley, with a long history of success in the US special services, somewhat tarnished in the last two years by the street cunning and relentless actions of the Cuban security, the impertinent and ubiquitous G-2 of Major Barbaroja. The other, Rafael Quintero, known among his friends as Chi-Chi, with less professional mileage but with very good relations with the anti-Castro movement and a proven loyalty to the Agency since the initial days of that surreptitious —and not so much— war.

"Look, Ted, the first impression is good, four disenchanted and very frightened officers at the evidence that many of their comrades have been executed without consideration or are already rotting in prison".

"Have you detected a G-2 infiltrator?" Shackley almost took it for granted.

Rafael Quintero could be, when he wanted, very objective and clear in his statements, both in English and Spanish.

"That there can be an infiltrator among them? Of course, it wouldn't be the first time that it happened to us, in fact, it strikes me as weird that an officer dismissed from the rebel army, with the surname Avilés, was destined to run a fishing company with little boats and everything". —Rafael shrugged—. "Do we have any evidence of that? No, negative, and we have investigated these men with people who know them, both down there and here".

Shackley nodded and took his time.

"What we have here, Quintero, are two issues, two separate and distinct cases, although at first glance they don't seem like it".

He began to make drawings of sailboats and little waves in sequence with a blue ink fountain pen in a pad of wide ruled paper, another traditionalistic trait of Shackley.

"On the one hand, three Cuban deserters who can be more or less useful to us if they want to collaborate, in information analysis, photographic recognition, interviews, support of infiltrations and things like that, handling, of course, the minimum of classified information".

He drew a circle with a single stroke on the lined paper.

"They can even talk on the radio in the transmissions to Cuba and encourage more of them to desert, second order tasks that always leave revenues and don't jeopardize our operations".

Shackley ripped the sheet of paper, crumpled it into a little ball and threw it into the waste basket.

Quintero nodded.

"On the other hand, we have the case of Captain Markis". —He traced an X in the new blank sheet—. "That man cannot in any way stay in Miami, they could even kill him here. Nor can he become, at all, Quintero, at all, a public figure".

The Cuban nodded again and said:

"And he has a rather repulsive past".

"He's a butcher, Rafael, but a butcher born in this country".

Shackley shook his head with studied slowness and said:

"One day that may have some practical utility, but far away from here". —He drummed the fingers of his right hand on the elegant desk—. "He was the executioner of an American and that is serious, but Morgan was a disgusting and troublesome man, who was with us and with others, or only with himself, God only knows!"

Quintero pursed his lips before talking again:

"I was wondering, Ted, about American law and that incident...

Shackley covered and uncovered his fountain pen now.

"You see, Commander Morgan, who sometimes seemed not being right in the head, resigned his citizenship in a moment of excitement". "Shackley sneezed and took a white handkerchief out of the back pocket of his pants to blow his nose, but not before placing the fountain pen very carefully on a leather square and blotting paper that covered a part of the desk—. "He fell in love with a Cuban woman and really believed that he was going to be a god there, amongst the Cubans. A very bad move on his part!"

"Yes, I've heard that before". —Rafael seemed to hesitate—. "What's more, I also heard that he worked for us, and for the New York Mafia, and for Castro himself as well, of course".

"He betrayed the Batistians that Trujillo sent through Trinidad, fools, and believed, Quintero, that with that Castro would leave him out of his control, to be on his own", he smiled. "Another clumsy assessment".

"You can't always be with both God and the Devil, you shouldn't", said the subordinate.

"Uh-huh!" —said the Boss and looked out the window as if appreciating the landscape, but everyone knew that the guy was making his decisions little by little and in sequence.

"That's why we must ignore this issue, Quintero, at least for the moment as if we were stupid and we didn't know. Besides, he, Markis, wasn't the one that condemned him to death, it was Castro, Markis did nothing more than to carry out an order given to him by his bosses at the moment, didn't he?", he smiled at Quintero.

"Yes, and there is no way to escape or to not comply with orders that come from above down there", added Quintero.

"They would have killed Morgan anyway and then take it out on

Markis, if he would have refused to shoot Morgan". —The American shrugged—. "He had no way to get away, he was in the wrong place at the wrong time, as they say".

"Yes, he could use that to his favor", Quintero was thoughtful for a few seconds and continued:

"If we push him, he will, he is not stupid, I have talked with him".

"Anyways, I think he knows he is in a trap. Or he accepts what we propose and he cooperates or he will have a lot of work rejoining the country where he was born".

"If he survives here".

"He will, but thanks to us".

"Do I pass him on to someone specific, to some other case officer?". the Agent asked.

"For now, separate him and his wife from the others". —The Boss thought for a moment—. "That 'friendship between comrades-in-arms' ended forever upon arriving to our shores".

Quintero nodded once more.

"I'm sure that he will accept any task anywhere so as not to have to live among exiled Cubans", the Director said.

"He would be crazy if he walked this streets", said Quintero.

"I don't think Markis is, like the unfortunate Commander Morgan, wrong in the head".

Ted Shackley gave a soft pat on the polished surface of the desk to indicate that the talk had ended.

"Okay Quintero, I'll ask Central and will tell you what to do with him". —He ripped the paper—. "With the others you do the same thing as always, and if anyone wants to go with relatives, if they have any here, let them, we have too many people here".

"Very well, boss".

"Go with God, son".

The Director smirked maliciously at him.

"And good luck".

6

BANGKOK, 1965

In the year 1965, Thailand, the enigmatic and inscrutable Siam from *The King and I*, a nation that could boast of not having been conquered by some foreign colonialist —though both the French and the English had snatched pieces of their territory some time ago—, was practically surrounded by a powder magazine about to explode, which was already being inflamed by three points at the same time although not well known yet for the Westerners, would soon become a constant presence in the popular speech: Vietnam, Laos and Cambodia.

Aware that this powder magazine and the rest of Southeast Asia, Thailand included, were in serious danger of falling into the hands of the indigenous communists supported by Mao's China and the Soviet Union, the United States had long been moving its economic, military and intelligence resources to the area.

Herman Markis, the young idealist who slid down the increasingly steep slope that began in the media and heroic rebellion of the bearded Cubans until he triumphantly arrived at the relentless, hard and real revolution, to then become an effective bureaucrat of summary executions and, thanks to these strange jumps that life usually gives, in January 1965, he came to be one of those military resources, now on the North American side, to Bangkok, 'the little town of the wild plum', the already enormous, labyrinthine and scattered imperial capital of great Thailand.

They landed, Anna and he, their bodies crushed by the long journey, and somewhat taken aback by the unknown, at the international airport of Bangkok, quite large and modern, but very far from what it would become in a few years.

Back in Miami, under the protection of JM WAVE, a verbal agreement was easily reached between Herman Markis and a CIA officer with an obviously fake name and apparently a lot of power, by which the latter was committed to help somehow: with some money, small amounts of food and clothing for Ana María's mother and sister who had remained in Cuba, who flatly denied to leave that mousetrap that was narrowing and moving farther outside of the western globe.

An agreement that was fulfilled under minimums —it seems that even held in good faith—, but couldn't be because the internal situation and security control on the island made it a little less than impossible. Besides it put in serious danger, for a very meager achievement and lacking operational sense, a human resource of the Company and to the interested parts, Ana and Gretel, there always was hope, and hope is the last thing that is lost.

Herman did what he could, and with very good will: nothing, nada.

After the agreement with the CIA, both Herman and Ana María were transferred within a few days to the city of Washington, where he joined a paramilitary training course at a base near the city and she began working as a cashier in a small grocery shop run by a married couple, her, Polish, he, an Italian, and to study English in the evenings. They lived in a small apartment in the Seven Corners suburb, across the Potomac River, in the city of Arlington, one of those beautiful housing conglomerates that surrounds the capital.

From their tiny balcony they could see the rolling hills of the National Cemetery and beyond, crossing the river, the Washington Monument, the long expanse of the Mall and the white dome of the Capitol Building.

One Sunday, while sleet was falling and the low light of day began to decline, Herman, standing behind the windows, while waiting for Ana to finish dressing and wrapping up warmly to go down to eat something and have a few beers, he wondered, looking in the vast cemetery the blurred thousands and thousands of aligned white crosses, sinuous and perfect, under how many of them were a shot soldier, executed by any banality that in times of peace wouldn't go any farther than of a simple scolding or an insignificant insult.

But Ana's animated voice cut the thread of those thoughts, mental speculations that didn't do him good and it was time to leave them in

38

a past that increasingly seemed more distant and out of place.

In that apartment they took refuge for almost a year, being cold, sleeping little, loving themselves like crazy and out of control, discovering new and exciting wet mucous areas that they didn't know they had in their bodies —although, still trying sporadically, it was difficult to cum outside to avoid the pregnancy, as he said, of Ana—, and watching on television, when they could, which wasn't common, the phenomenon of the Beatles touring the United States, congressional fights and in the streets, Johnson's Civil Rights Act and in November the presidential election in which Lyndon Johnson himself, Kennedy's unexpected heir, smashed Republican Senator Barry Goldwater, a right-winger which people jokingly claimed that he wanted to reestablish slavery.

Christmas day of 1964, colder than before, were a mixture of dazzling, happiness and contained pain, especially for Ana María who lived with a tight heart for those who had remained in Cuba and of which she heard from very little, in fact, almost nothing.

On New Year's Day, 1965 Ana found out about two things at the same time: Herman explained to her that they were going to a remote place, on the other side of the world for who knows how long, but that they would continue being together and improve their finances, thank God; and she also noticed from the nausea and lack of menstruation that she was pregnant.

"From now on, sex is over until the baby is born", Herman said in a doctoral tone.

"*Nanay*, love, don't be stupid, it won't harm anybody if we do it well!"

But being left behind because of her motherhood? No way. Her man was her man and one had to follow him wherever he went, to the end of the world, just as she said in an unforgettable afternoon for her and for him, on the Cuban beach of Guanabo.

Bangkok, a gigantic and sprawling city, though disconcerting and disturbing to the uninitiated, turned out to be far less threatening than it seemed.

They occupied a small apartment in a modern ten-story building inhabited almost entirely by officials from the US embassy or other western legations, located in the Watthana district, a few blocks away from low but spacious and highly functional buildings, surrounded by sports fields, which housed what they all called The American School of Bangkok.

Ana was, a couple of weeks after settling in, accepted —someone or something unknown recommended her to the management of the school— as an assistant in the library of the American School of Thailand, a cozy place where they spoke and learned English, which was very much like a well-educated educational institution in the United States, with the difference that students, almost all of them children of diplomats, military attaches, trade representatives, managers of international companies and bankers, or other more heterodox and mysterious occupations, came from the four cardinal points of the planet, resulting in a picturesque variety of languages, forms of dress, culinary tastes and characters.

From North Americans, of course, to Indians, Belgians, Germans and Portuguese, Chileans and Swedes, Australians, Taiwanese, Argentinians, Swiss, Mexicans and a myriad of human specimens, a rainbow of nationalities. Really a very interesting place and of easy socialization as long as there was not much research on the parental and even maternal activities, of the students.

There were still no Cubans there, Ana was the first, but the political commotions of the distant island, the successive exoduses, the success and business expansion and the Indochinese wars that were to come would bring mor Cubans in a future that was not far off, it was just around the corner.

What was clear in the School was that tuition was expensive, resources were plentiful and teachers and administrators were well paid.

What more could you ask for?

In fact, and that seemed to Ana a kind of miracle, a teacher from Canada with whom she got along very well —they were about the same age and their respective husbands were military officers with unclear functions and long periods of absence—, had a sister who worked at the Canadian embassy in Havana, to whom it wasn't so hard, as long as it was done with great discretion, to provide some groceries and some money to Gretel.

In a few days, Herman joined his new job as a Police Aerial Resupply Unit (PARU) instructor, a paramilitary unit of the Thai political police created years ago with covert and generally quite questionable functions, as it were, but necessary if one wanted to prevent communists and anti-monarchist rebels from gaining ground and strength in those lands.

Ana, didn't know the details, of course, for her, her husband worked as an instructor of the Imperial Army within the framework of the North American development aid, and that was enough. Or should suffice.

She was concerned only with two things: her husband's physical integrity —there was already open talks about American casualties in Southern Vietnam and where and how easy the child inside her was going to be born.

The other thing, her mother and her brother and sister were no longer a concrete and obvious concern, they were only a dull, bearable pain that was exacerbated when she was surrounded by too much peace.

That's why being stunned by the adaptation to the new environment worked very well, to settle and make the house beautiful, improve her English and a job well done.

Time heals.

So they say.

7

U TAPAO AIR BASE, 1965

By road, the trip from the southern suburbs of Bangkok to Pattaya —crossing the crowded capital from one end to the other might take quite some time— can be done in about two and a half hours, depending on the quality of the vehicle, the time of day or night, and that no serious accidents, truck breakdowns or other incidents, such as elephants or oxen walking meekly along the road, obstruct free transit.

In 1965 Pattaya was already advertised as a foreigner friendly beach town, a resort with very good food, both Thai and international, friendly and smiling people, many entertainment and even some unconventional venues, and moral and sexual codes as flexible as a Japanese contortionist, in short, a little corner to spend two or three days in a big way, for decent families as well as for the degenerate, of all kinds, and for prices quite affordable to the average pocket.

By leaving Pattaya behind and following Highway #3 —Sukhumvit Road— to the south and then to the southeast, one will arrive, in about forty-five or fifty minutes, to Phla Rayong, a rather nondescript and not very populated area, with rice fields, palms, mesquite trees, enormous ebonies scattered throughout the field, some kalule rubber trees here and there, abundant vegetation and green sections, oxen grazing or attached to the yoke and mangroves in the distance, a reminder of the proximity of the low waters of the north bend of the Thailand or Siam Gulfs, a liquid finger that enters the country like the exploratory index of a proctologist.

There, at Phla Rayong, leaving the #3 route and taking a secondary road but in good condition one suddenly encounters the fences and watch towers of the U Tapao Air Base, one of the five or six military installations that the Americans built in those parts of the Thai territory at that time, with which they predicted, with great accuracy, that they would become critical storage points for fuel and ammunition, interdiction and support operations, equipment repair and other decisive tasks for the gigantic air campaigns to come over the entire Indochinese sky.

But U Tapao was destined to grow larger than the others and to become the most important North American Air Base in Asia —excepting perhaps the formidable Kadena Air Base in Okinawa, Japan, and the Osan Air Base in South Korea—, to house the wings of B-52s and fast F-111s that would mercilessly crush, with a debatable and relative efficacy, both South and North Vietnam, the so-called Ho Chi Minh Route, Laos and Cambodia as the war was starting to get out of control in the years to come.

Instructor Herman Markis didn't arrive on a January morning to U Tapao to fly planes but to be integrated as an adviser —the Thais are very jealous of their ranks and headquarters— of a PARU platoon called *Crash Site*, men who, at least in theory, had to arrive to the remote places where a plane or a helicopter —friend or foe, legal or illegal— fell to rescue survivors, count and pack corpses, take photographs, collect interesting material and *safeguard* all possible information that could improve the Intel of the Kingdom's Army and, incidentally, that of the US Army and US Intelligence Agencies.

Of course, other missions were carried out, especially in the intricate regions prone to subversion and in the relatively close and poorly defended Cambodia. But those tasks were secretive and silent for Cambodia was a sovereign and allied country at the time, and it was supposed that friends don't violate the privacy nor borders of the other however porous they may be.

Already Herman was beginning to get bored after a couple of weeks of long and tiring day walks through the woods. The almost constantly soaked grasslands and the coastal mangroves, tormented all the time by the rains, fortunately not as furious as in summer, and mosquitoes, gnats and other bugs whose names he had not yet time to learn, to then laze before the sunset and the hot and abundant ranch and then lay on the bunk beds until dawn.

Unexpectedly —finally, at last!—, the order came to move the platoon. About fifteen men to a place that would be told on the way.

In a couple of jeeps and a truck they drove to the Rayong district, a little further west from where Highway #3 intersects with 36, and guided by an inhabitant of the area, obviously a police informant, left the vehicles behind and entered, on foot and in a separate single file, by paths in the forest that took them to an area of small wooded hills.

The commands of the communist guerrillas that were proliferating more and more in neighboring countries were obsessed with penetrating Thailand, and the Thai military government —King Bhumibol Adulyadej, revered also as Rama IX and known as the one-eyed who by the way was born in the United States, was actually a figure of worship, decorative, not to give out orders or be obeyed— was obsessed with preventing it at all costs.

It was simply an operation of elimination and cleaning of a squalid group that aspired to be a guerrilla, some wretches playing war and, of course, obtaining people that informed about their contacts and possible suppliers.

The task itself, though it was necessary to walk a lot and sweat a lot in that fucking jungle, lasted no more than half an hour.

The eight or nine guerrillas, some beardless youths, or so they seemed, were caught from several sides at the same time and any possibility of escape was cut silently and professionally.

Three or four were shot to death in a desperate attempt to resist and the rest, after running around a little, gave themselves up as prisoners, whining, making a fuss and clamoring for their lives.

Of the interrogation —bad, bad news for the poor captured devils, that bitterness of being interrogated— and analysis of the information obtained would be commissioned another PARU group specialized in those dark tasks.

But what Herman didn't know was that that day, right there, would be his fire test before the Thai paramilitaries.

As a foreign advisor he could avoid it, because his job was to guide, teach, and not kill, but if he didn't, if he showed that he was not up to the roughness and coldness of the men he accompanied, his work, endorsed by the prestige of the hard, henceforth, would be nothing less than useless.

He understood immediately, instinctively, that this was an unwritten initiation ritual by the PARU groups who had to swallow, without saying a word, the foreign advisors, or else, pick up their stuff and leave.

As they were leaving, they walked unhurriedly to a clear savanna where a Choctaw H-34 helicopter would pick them up, a flying piece of junk with visible rust, spasmodic vibrations and with more flying hours than the years that Methuselah had, but where they all fit: the whole platoon and the prisoners... except one, as the son of a bitch Thai fox who commanded the platoon told him.

"He doesn't fit, he's too heavy", the man said with a cynical, brazen smile.

Herman looked at him from above, the bastard was short, and was about to order him to go on foot, or to hell, but he restrained himself.

The one that didn't fit in the helicopter —to Herman's eyes a skinny, filthy little China-man with his hands tied behind his back with a hemp rope and his gaze straying behind the little eyes who didn't weighed even a hundred pounds— was standing not knowing exactly what was happening, but behind those expressionless faces one never knew in truth what they knew or reasoned about.

In his bureaucratic years, as he asserted, Herman had never been part of a firing squad as a shooter. His work had always consisted in directing the squad of riflemen from the side —the usual ready, aim... fire— and give the shot of grace, or shots, sometimes one didn't achieve its objective.

Invariably the loser, the man he shot in the head, was already dead or so battered by the bullets of five or six combat rifles that he didn't even realize what he would do to him. On a few occasions, the guy moved and complained or even, a couple of times, begged, between spasms and mouthfuls of blood, to end it once and for all.

The recurring nightmare that woke him in a sweat and that Ana had learned to calm with her embraces was of a strong, dour, silent mulatto, a former Batista government policeman, who came to the wall walking without allowing anyone to touch him. He stood up straight, as if he had a stick up his ass, and rudely spat toward the six little soldiers who made up the firing squad.

Herman had learned that with guys like that it was best to speed up the process, especially when the members of the executing squad were too young or too new to the task.

The condemned man received the closed discharge in full at his torso —even white smoke came out in two or three places of the clumsy inmate clothes— and fell on his butt with a sound like a sack-cloth. And there he stayed, his hands resting on the uneven, stony, dirty floor of the fort's den, as blood spurted from the wounds in his chest and belly.

When Herman approached to put an end to that terror the guy looked at him with a glassy, deep and disproportionate hate and he spat again, this time without much force. Herman, slowly, turned around him and shot him almost at the nape of the neck, but the bullet unexpectedly hit him on the left shoulder. The man leaned forward, then straightened up again and patted the ground with the urgency of someone who wants something but doesn't get it. And yes, he stayed, to Herman's and to the surprise of the whole platoon, in the same position, sitting.

Herman squeezed the trigger again and inconceivably the bullet, a reinforced 45-caliber projectile, snatched a piece of his left ear and made a groove in his face and nothing else. The mulatto tried to stand up babbling something like a prayer or a litany in a strange and cave-dwelling language, indecipherable to Herman.

He couldn't stand, though he tried, so he struck the earth again with his palms, with a vehemence similar to that of the Rumberos hitting a flamenco drum box or a *tumbadora*.

What the hell was that!?

Then, in the perplexity of all present, a member of the platoon, a skinny and scrawny black man with his oversized olive-green uniform, in violation of the military rules of silence and order, shouted to Herman:

"Captain, *por su madre*, remove the *safeguard*, remove it!"

Herman didn't understand what the man meant and surely the bewilderment and confusion were visible at a distance.

"Captain, Captain, permission to help you!", the soldier shouted again.

Herman, completely overwhelmed by what was happening, didn't authorize nor prevent it, simply because he had no idea what to say or do.

The black man came out of formation without waiting any longer and in seven or eight swift strides he traveled the gravel space that separated him from the place where the mulatto was sitting on the floor, bleeding, hitting the floor with his hands and reciting his unintelligible litany, invocation or whatever the hell it was.

Herman stared with his mouth open like a fish, unable to assert his authority, holding in his hand a weapon that seemed to have lost its lethal deadly power against this unarmed and defenseless person, but obviously, and against all odds, alive.

Ignoring Herman, who was watching him do it, the black man put his FAL rifle on his back, crouched with agility, avoiding to look at the dying man's face, wrapped his bony hands around his neck and yanked off, with strength, a kind of metal chain that didn't look like gold, with a hessian sack while he made the sign of the cross over his head and recited a little prayer, or request, in a language that wasn't Spanish, but which it resembled much, or was the same litany that the man recited.

"Shoot him now, shoot him, Captain, don't make him suffer any more!" —Asked the black man and he ran back to the group of shooters, who watched, paralyzed with astonishment, throwing with force the thing that he yanked from the man's neck as far as he could.

"Shoot him, Captain, *por su madre*, shoot him now!", the man repeated.

Herman, barely controlling the trembling of his hand, shot without aiming and the mulatto fell round to one side, stiff as a stick, dead.

Although the last projectile that Herman put in the nape of the man's neck had come out of the side, disengaging his lower jaw a little, the face of the deceased showed peace, a tranquility that was inexplicable considering everything he had suffered to end up going to the other side or wherever those who died went.

Then, in the sleeping tent, the members of the execution platoon and other soldiers gave him a drink directly from a bottle of cheap rum. Herman needed it, and explained to him that a *safeguard* is a 'job', a 'work' made by the priest of an Afro-Cuban religion to a believer, in this case the mulatto condemned to death, to preserve his life of all evil that could threaten him.

The *safeguard* was made out of human bones, the remains of certain animals, herbs, seeds and other materials offered to an orisha —a saint—, who was responsible for providing protection to the believer after a long and varied secret ceremony.

That work, of course, had been done to him a long time before, and no one, by ignorance, had thought to remove it from the neck when they caught him and condemned him to die.

When Herman told him, without many details, to the man in black beret, still under the impression of astonishment that it caused him, the latter said with an indisputable remnant of contempt, from the shield of his usual ideological superiority and arrogance:

"Bullshit, Herman, and don't be a comemierda, don't ever let those in the platoon to step on you..." He was lighting a cigar and looking at him sideways.

"Or is it that you no longer have the balls to make this simple job?"

Herman apologized, blamed the incident on his ignorance of the idiosyncrasy of Cuban blacks and didn't tell him what he had on the tip of his tongue:

"How easy it is to chew me out here in the office, but what the fuck would you have done in that case?"

But all that was far behind, except in his recurring nightmares.

With a calmness that he didn't feel, Herman walked slowly to the boy and pointed a finger at a distant point on the other side of the helicopter, indefinitely away.

He had the fleeting idea that he was pointing to God. Which god?

The noise of the engine was deafening and the air displaced by the blades whipping the faces made everything more messy and confusing.

When the boy turned his head, as if stunned, trying to understand what he was supposed to see in that place he hadn't still located, Herman put, almost like a reflex, a bullet behind his right ear with his regulation Colt. 45.

The body jumped in the air, first up and in a split second fell forward as if a battering ram had struck it.

He shifted his leg convulsively and then was completely still.

Herman ran to the helicopter that was already peeling the smooth rubber of the undercarriage off from the leaf littered on the ground. Two pairs of heavy hands helped him up and he jumped and jostled among the soldiers that, although he didn't understand what they were saying obviously they were already talking and laughing at other things that had nothing to do with the unavoidable spoils, which remained in the earth like food to the carrion birds.

Black birds that were already circling the sky.

Waiting.

8

Royal Thai Air Force Hospital, 1965

Ana María, with a huge eight months pregnant belly and an uncomfortable swelling in the ankles and legs, apart from persistent back pain, was unable to fly twenty or more hours to Washington. Besides, to be in whose company?

Herman, the only person she had in this world, could have accompanied her in the last two or three weeks but it wasn't advisable to go so far. That's why they finally decided, after doubts and daily changing of mind, that the delivery was going to be in Bangkok and whatever God willed. And what God willed was that a PARU instructor just like him but with several years of experience in those lands talked with Herman, while they had a couple of beers in the base mess hall, of a female Thai obstetrician —wife of a North American Ranger's Colonel—, who had studied medicine and made her specialty in some hospital, he didn't know which one, in the United States.

Just by asking the husband of that doctor, a very big, somewhat old guy who looked like John Wayne with white hair and a thick belly, and who was a living myth among special forces men and paratroopers, but also a very accessible jokester. So, they both went looking for him.

"Let my wife take care of your wife!" —The American put his bear-like arm over Herman's shoulders—. "But that will cost you a round of beers, young man".

Easy peasy.

Dr. Sirikit —by the way, it's the same name as the Empress of Thailand—, worked in the Obstetrics Department of the Royal Hospital of the Thai Air Force. The Royal Hospital was, and it still is, a solid, u-shaped and ugly but very well-conditioned building located in Sai Mai, on the northern outskirts of the capital, just opposite the Don

Mueang Airport, separated only by the Motorway #1 linking Bangkok with the central plateau, the city of Chiang Mai, the highlands and No Man's Land of the Golden Triangle, the black hole of the international opium trade.

Small, nice without being pretty (Thais are not usually good-looking to Western standards but they have other values that lure those who know them well), nervous, extremely competent, fairly bossy and dominant with her subordinates, Doctor Sirikit turned out to be, more than a doctor, a wise adviser and, after some time, a good friend.

She told Ana of her loneliness and startles in the United States, where she didn't know anybody and didn't fluently understand the language, when she arrived with her husband, an adventurous soldier, drinker and womanizer whom she had met at the time of the Korean War, and whom she had tamed with that wise love, perseverance and strength of character that years later would make two other Asian women very famous, also bossy and autocratic, but extraordinarily sagacious: Imelda Marcos and Yoko Ono.

In the end, after giving birth to several children to the American, she had finally dragged him back to her country, Thailand, where she expected that him, considerably older than her, to retire soon from active service.

"Although these fools never completely retire", she said to Ana, smiling mischievously. "They think they'll get rid of us that way!"

And also hoping that they would grow old together watching from the balcony of her pretty apartment the Chao Phraya River run into the sea at dusk, and buying herself fresh groceries —the kitchen was part of her charm— in the floating markets of the canals, which, although they smelled bad, and when she said that she laughed heartily, they were the channels of her city, which she had learned to love as a child.

The story had many similarities Ana's own, but Ana doubted that her own story had a conclusion as happy and peaceful as promised by Dr. Sirikit.

In order to avoid car trips in the hellish streets and roads of Bangkok, the doctor admitted Ana, exaggerating the problem of the edemas and the increase of the blood pressure, several days before birth. And whenever she had some free time, passed by her room, in the officers wing of the hospital, to talk for a while, give her candy that she would later forbid in her medical indications and to also lift her spirits.

"How's it going with the cubanita and cubanito we're waiting?"

"You're the one who knows how we're doing, Doctor". —And Ana smiled, relieved that someone would offer her the security and strength that often escaped her.

"You have to get rid of all the salt and sugar from your diet". —She pointed admonishingly with her finger as she opened the drawer of her nightstand and dropped a pair of Swiss chocolates.

"At your service, Dr. Sirikit!" —And Ana saluted.

One early morning —the doctor began to visit the women in labor at dawn— she placed, next to the tiny gold crucifix that Gretel carried everywhere in Cuba, a jade carved Buddha.

"It's for the good luck of the cubanita and cubanito". —She raised her index finger in the air in warning—. "Don't thank me".

"What do I do then?"

"Nothing". —She pinched her forearm—. "Rest and sleep like all good girls".

Those were days of hope, but also of depressive evocations of her mother, now turned enemy and probably unfamiliar and disinterested in the fact that soon she would be a grandmother; of her sister Gretel, sacrificed, immolated by everybody's selfishness; of her jailed brother, whom she sometimes could scarcely remember in detail, which frightened and filled her with senseless but oppressive remorse.

In the afternoons, especially in the darkening torrential rains, furious, thick winds typical of that strange country, Ana wondered what the hell was she doing there, thousands of miles from her home and her city, tied to the fate of a man she loved very much and whom she wanted almost like the first day, now with more tenderness and less outburst, but of whom she knew almost nothing. A man who disappeared for weeks, she knew that he was a fatherless orphan, that he had a hippie mother who had a little boy from another man, somewhere in California and that they would one-day visit, when things eventually returned to normal, if they ever returned.

The belly was growing lower and sharper, her lower back was split with pain and she didn't want to know of anything else except food, that's why she dreamed of a bowl of prime ground meat with white rice, raisins and olives, like the ones her mother cooked in the good old days that would never return.

"I'm going to burst, Doctor!"

"Ha! You should have seen me in my second pregnancy". —Sirikit gave a little jump and sat down, violating her own rules, on the edge of the bed—. I looked like a spindle, a toad's belly, with a little head on top, and my two thin legs underneath.

"But I can't take it anymore!"

"Of course, you can, cubanite. —And kept on walking towards the door.

Ana broke water in the sleep of a quiet night.

Herman, who got along well with his bosses and was on leave, accompanied her, frightened and stiff, that morning which was forecasted to be —strangely enough— fresh and sunny, to the delivery room, where Dr. Sirikit ceased to be the friend –these transformations were part of her personality and occurred without apparent transitions– to turn into the scrupulous and effective professional who always dominated, like a Troop General, the stage, her personal battlefield.

Ana, a Cuban woman with a robust pelvis and wide hips, both exercised in her usual walks and bringing happiness to her man, her male, gave birth to a seven-pound kid who bellowed almost immediately as he went out to the world.

Dr. Sirikit patted the newborn's slim buttocks with her little but stiff hand like a whip, lifted him up in the air and said something in Thai that Ana didn't understand and Herman guessed it was a kind of blasphemy. She placed the red little thing on the saucer of a dumbbell, wiped his face, looked with deft gestures at the hole in his ass and the tiny, wrinkled testicles, did something with the umbilical cord and gave a couple of orders to the helpers.

She turned to Ana and Herman with the child in her hands.

The doctor showed him to the frightened parents as an offering.

"The *fucking* cubanito!"

"A cubanazo!, said Herman.

"And half American!" —Ana let out with a tired sigh of relief.

Sirikit wrapped the newborn in a green cloth and placed him on Ana's breast.

"Congratulations! He's healthy".

Ana was crying.

"Why are you crying, Ana?", asked Herman.

"Because I'm an idiot!" —She curled up beside Herman's arm, looking at the boy with a flush—. It's nothing, Herman, nothing.

And now they were three.

Ana thought of the late Rubino, of Ana Donremí, of Máximo, of her little sister, Gretel, the girl with the sullen face and the heart of gold.

And she cried.

And she wept with shrieking and soul.

9

LONG TIENG BASE, 1967

For legal purposes, Herman Rubino Markis (without Santana, the mother's surname is not used amongst Anglo-Saxons, hence the joke that they have no mother) had been registered in the consular office of the American Embassy in Bangkok as an American citizen born in a military base of that country, which in fact hadn't been so, because the hospital of the air force in which the birth took place is property and territory of the Thai Kingdom, but who cared of such nonsense in that moment?

The child grew up healthy and trilingual as Ana took care of the Spanish, Herman of English when he was around, and the nana, Suyin, of Thai.

They had consulted with Dr. Sirikit about the possibility that Ana would return to the United States to raise the child there, but the doctor, a wise and practical woman, had reasoned that there, in Bangkok, Ana had already a small circle of friends, that it was much easier and cheap to get help for the house work and of nurturing and that she had a job that pleased her and filled her loneliness in which her husband —she knew about that!— put her in with his absence.

–Why do such madness? –She said while decorating a pumpkin pudding Thai style that she would offer as dessert after an sumptuous food served on the terrace of her apartment in front of the river–. What will she do alone, with a newborn, in that big, cold, unfriendly America? And don't you worry about nationality, that could be fixed here. —She said it matter-of-factly—. My children are all Americans, although one of them was born here.

And the two of them, Ana and Herman, after thinking about it a little more and hearing some other opinions, had agreed with Dr. Sirikit's reasons.

"In a way, this is a lot more like Cuba", Herman told Ana sometime.

"Yeah, yeah, it's possible", Ana answered without much conviction.

They reciprocated the invitation to the doctor and her husband to communicate their decision, and Herman to ensure their protection against any possible harm that might happen to Ana and the child. Ana María took care, under the tutelage of Suyin, to prepare a meal up to the guests standards:

Tomyam Plamuk, a spicy soup that Herman evaded as much as possible and that the colonel ate twice; savoring some fish cakes (Tod Man) seasoned with tamarind sauce that the four did enjoy; Kai Muang as the main dish —what a way to eat, God!—; and Toi Shell as salad; fruit, especially papaya prepared in various forms and American chocolate ice cream. All that with Singha beer for the ladies and Scotch whiskey for the gentlemen. Oh, and to top it all, a rare and old Porto brought by the Colonel from his private cellar, gathered through the years with the pleasure and sophistication of good drinkers.

At the table, the colonel, feeling his protruding belly, declared:

"Or we bring Ana to live with us to cook for us —he winked—, "or they lend us that girl, Suyin I think she's called, from time to time".

It had been more than two years since the hesitations and doubts about their residency had been left behind, and life, once more, had proved the doctor right.

The previous year the three had flown to Washington via the Philippines and San Francisco. Little Herman was already walking and they paid a seat for him in a commercial airline with the idea that the child would visit his country for the first time and Ana would regularize his citizenship in the United States. A few days later the baby was crying for Suyin, and Ana was missing the routine of her work, her friendships and her calm life in Bangkok, except, of course, the uncertainty that gripped her thinking about Herman and his strange war.

Eventually, Herman's absences would increase, as he was destined to logistically support the Hmong rebels, a rare, tough, tiny Laotian tribe with distant historical roots in China and northern Thailand, who fought fiercely the North Vietnamese invaders and the pro-Communist government of Laos, which they didn't consider it their government but the assailant who was taking away their rice and opium.

For several months Herman was training commandos of Hmong guerrillas, both in the highlands of Thailand and in the Laotian mountains, but the extent of the attacks of the regular North Vietnamese army, which combined with an unprecedented increase in the movement of troops all over the Ho Chi Minh Route and the continued offensive of the Viet Cong in South Vietnam were about to destabilize the whole area and put an end to the North American strategy on the Indochinese Peninsula.

In northern Laos, between the capital Vientiane and the enigmatic Plain of Jars, both somewhat further south and the porous border with North Vietnam —Porous? Wide open— to the west, the Americans had an Agency base officially called —officially it didn't exist in any document or report but almost everyone knew it was there—: Lima Site 20A (the A came from *alternative*), which was in an inter-mountain valley more than three thousand feet high that appeared on maps with the name of Long Tieng.

Long Tieng, or Lima Site 20A, had become a gigantic operation of the Agency and its special forces, with a long main landing strip and a few secondary strips, clearings in the jungle for helicopters, protective casemates and elevated observation posts, office bungalows, barracks, covered kitchens and roofed mess halls, emergency medical services, warehouses, powder magazines and all the facilities that a Headquarter might need. Although under the appearance of a military base of the pro-Western government of Laos.

And if all that wasn't enough, it was covered, day and night, by a «civilian» airline that could be considered its own, Air America —which jokers called Air Opium— that had been working since the mythical times of General Chennault and his famous Flying Tigers in the difficult and distant years of the war against the Japanese.

Once, flying in an old Dakota C-47 —the best airplane ever made, or so they say— from the Thai border base of Nakhon to Long Tieng, twenty minutes in the air if all was well, Herman settled himself down as best he could —the cockpit was loaded with mortar .88 rounds and boxes of shells of different calibers, even live chickens in cages—next to a guy with a thin mustache who said to him, after looking at him sideways for a while:

"Hey, *chico*, you speak Spanish?"

Herman shook and replied in English to the man:

"I understand a little since I was in Mexico, why?"

The mustachioed guy then told Herman, in perfect English, that he had been in a Cuban jail for almost two of years after being taken prisoner during the Bay of Pigs invasion, in which he had participated as a paratrooper. There, the prisoners, in the absence of an armed intervention by the American Marines, were expecting to be killed or rot for decades in the dungeons of Castro, but the gringo money and a load of preserves and farm implements had radically altered the landscape.

"Your face seemed familiar from that time, from some prison or something, but no, it must have been someone like you".

"Could be", Herman shrugged.

Although forbidden, the unknown man lit a cigarette smugly, turned off the match by shaking his hand and tossed it still smoking under the seat.

"They say we all have a double, right? And you're that guy's double", he went on.

"I'm from California and have never been in Cuba", Herman replied, turning down the cigarette the guy was offering him and pointed at the red forbidden signal and the wooden boxes and straps with .50-caliber machine-gun shells.

The guy ignored the warning as if it wasn't for him:

"I'm sorry, *brother*, but the world's so small". —He laughed heartily and patted Herman's right shoulder—. Don't worry about the explosives, *chico*, one must die of something, we have more risk of dying perched on this flying thing that they no longer use even in Cuba, don't you think?

Herman, who had had time to recover, nodded in a studied calm.

Fortunately for Herman they landed minutes later, smoothly.

The man, almost certainly a postman from the Agency, was out of sight after the landing, not without first saying good-bye to him with the characteristic Cuban effusiveness.

"See you soon, *mi hermano,* much luck to you, and keep a watchful eye, these chinamen don't trust even their own mothers!", he patted his back.

"Take care of yourself too, *chiiiico!*"

They both laughed heartily.

That meeting left him brooding and somewhat haggard all day. What did his previous history matter if his bosses, those who were in command of the Agency, knew it perfectly. What did it matter, but something had to make his consciousness uneasy when he denied that he had been, and something more, in that little island that sometimes seemed so distant and somewhat alien.

Human beings, that mammal in clothes as a ranger has said a little maddened, totally toasted, with whom he had coincided in a punishment mission in Cambodia, was a strange being, he could kill with fury his equals, and at the same time he allowed himself to be killed with an unthinkable passivity.

When he fought with the guerrillas of the man in the black beret in Cuba, they would gag the pigs that were going to be stabbed to roast and eat them, so that their hideous grunts and howlings would not betray their position to the enemy, nevertheless, he had never had to gag a condemned man who was to be executed. Sometimes they shouted a slogan against Communism or gave some prayer to their God, but shouting or screaming, never.

The mulatto of his nightmares had stopped before the firing squad, and, besides from spitting, he had done nothing. He could have screamed, shrieked, ran, could have attacked him and even taken his weapon —the fellow, a *fucking* forced visit of his night visions, was much more burly than he—, so he could have killed him if he had wanted, but no, he had just stood there —like a man, like a macho Herman said to himself— and waited for him to be shot with impunity until he was destroyed. And so they all did, one after another, night after night.

We always defend ourselves from our past, as I did on the plane today, and we almost never defend ourselves when others decide to kill us, or, as that bastard in the black beret said, to execute us, he thought.

The mustachioed guy had made him philosophical, morose, rather.

But by the next day, very busy since long before dawn, he had almost erased the Cuban and all that nonsense from his mind.

Things got complicated and a whirlwind of unknown dimensions was rising right in front of everyone's eyes. In Washington, in the Agency, in the Pentagon, everyone, everyone was smiling in public and talking, as always, of confidence, of an assured victory, but the truth was that they were getting more nervous and scared.

Unbelieving the impossibility of finishing once and for all those fucking *chinitos*.

In denial.

These were no longer small interdiction operations or penetrations into more or less enemy territory. Now it was a life or death open war.

And that war was not being done to win it, that war was going to be lost, and everyone understood as much because it was a splendid and costly blunder.

"For God's sake, a screw up!"

"A *fucking* screw up!"

10

Lima Site 85, 1968

Buddhism prevails among Laotians, but it's hard to find one who at the same time does not believe in *phi*, the spirits which are thousands and can do much good, provide health and prosperity, calmness to the soul. Especially if they are respected as they deserve and are given the due homage. They can be evil just the same, depending on their essence, their temperament and perverse condition, or if they are simply underestimated or offended.

The cult of ancestors, so rooted in all Asia, has much of that animism that also invokes the *phi*. Without ancestors we wouldn't exist, therefore, a powerful or rich man, a victorious warrior, a wise teacher, a famous politician or a good and spontaneous being wouldn't have existed without ancestors and, therefore, those ancestors must be object of homage and remembrance.

Talking about descendants to come is a waste of time, we are the present and we exist thanks to the ancestors, the future is a nonsense that may or may not arrive, or arrive in a very different way than we think or want.

As a brave, and peculiarly cruel Hmong chief told Herman after a long exchange of opinions, sitting on a log and in front of a boiling tea with aromatic leaves, talking about tactics of war and of respect which was not usually had, to the life of prisoners:

"When you westerners talk about what your children will be you waste time, but when you insult someone by pointing to him that he is a son of a bitch, you're right, because that bitch mother, if she really was or is, is an ancestor, and to insult ancestors does offend".

For them, the Laotians (also for Thais, Cambodians and many Vietnamese), the *phi* dwell in things, in springs, in rivers, in fire and its embers, in the great trees, in the mountains, in nature, in short, everywhere. But there are privileged places where great and powerful *phi* dwell, or damned places where evil spirits or tormented souls dwell, that when their bodies die violently or tragically, they can't reincarnate, and they suffer, and they make mortals suffer.

Phou Pha Thi is a fantastically beautiful and almost inaccessible mountain peak of the central Indochinese mountain range, located in the part of that extensive mountain range that runs through Lao territory, and with two striking characteristics.

The first one is that it is just over a hundred miles, in a straight line from Hanoi (some said that 85, the site number, was the correct figure in miles, but there might be an error or some misinformation in that) the capital of North Vietnam and the command center of all subversion on the Indochinese peninsula. In other words, the house, the home of Uncle Ho and his military brain, the silent, cunning and always humble General Giap.

And the second is that in it there are supposed to inhabit important *phi*, (the Laotians don't suppose, they are more than certain) so, it is a sacred mountain whose peace shouldn't be desecrated by the endless and often absurd human quarrels.

Precisely in this near-square cliff, with walls cut to a peak of 200 or more meters of free fall, taking into account its relative proximity to Hanoi, the command of the American Air Force decided to install a *tactical air navigation system*, TACAN —to say it in the specialists code language—, which is nothing more than a very powerful radar capable of guiding, from one place to another, many aircrafts at the same time. That said, the USAF asked the Agency to operate and protect it, but with the necessary secrecy so that the North Vietnamese wouldn't discover it, which they would obviously try to destroy it at any cost. Nor the western journalists and diplomats, as Laos was supposed to have their neutrality respected.

It was a time when there were still no reconnaissance and control satellites and anti-aircraft defenses made it difficult to fly radar planes in the areas near the zones that were to be bombed, so it was necessary to have a TACAN as close as possible to Hanoi. And Phou Pha Thi, the sacred mountain, was precisely that place.

And although the Agency took the request willingly, let's not forget that Agency men are like old dogs, you can't teach them new tricks, in turn they requested the Air Force an officer that could take care of the important aspect of the link between the TACAN operators and the squadrons of bombers and their protection fighters directly on the battlefield.

That man was the E-9 (*Chief Master Sergeant*) Richard Etchberger, Etch for his associates, not only one of the best and most experienced ground operations officers, but the best the USAF could count on. And the CIA man in charge of organizing the defense that the Hmong guerrillas and a company of the Thai royal army would offer —there shouldn't be, by any means, American combat troops involved— couldn't be other than Herman Markis, to whom the Hmong respected and particularly recognized his value.

Herman had been careful to develop a perimeter defensive system that would withstand the thrust of a relatively large guerrilla force and have time, in an extreme case, to destroy the technical equipment and withdraw the American specialists and the Hmong and Thai platoons to the west.

But that system was based, inevitably, on finding in time any major force that tried to approach Phou Pha Thi, and that had to be done by the air reconnaissance facilities of the USAF and the Agency.

On March 9th, 1978 Markis arrived for the umpteenth time in a gray Bell 204B helicopter with the insignia of Air America to the small clearing that operated as a landing strip at the edge of the cliffs, high as giant walls, of peak Phou Pha Thi.

To fool the West into the matter of the American presence in Laos was nothing, that was being done day by day for a long time, but trying to go unnoticed into Hanoi, who took care of its vital Ho Chi Minh route and its capital like the apple of its eye, and also had a whole army in Laos, Pathet Lao, could be described as a childlike desire, not to say a supreme stupidity, or worse, a sign of intolerable ineptitude.

As some funny soldier wrote on the wall of a military urinal: Ho Chi Minh doesn't suck his thumb, he sticks it to us every day up the ass!

Herman came to the place along with an American commander, both dressed in civilian clothes, to pick up the blondies, to dismantle the operation, to save what could be salvageable, and to finish that mad adventure in the best possible way.

There was a sense of urgency in the task, but no one thought it would be that much.

The whole perimeter of Phou Pha Thi was already under sporadic fire and it was known that North Vietnamese forces were approaching, but what they inexplicably didn't know, either the USAF or the Agency, or anyone else was that 3,000 selected North Vietnamese soldiers, including Special Force companies and mountain climbers were stationed in the forest, a few miles away and perfectly camouflaged, awaiting the order of attack, which arrived... the next day.

And in the early hours of the 9th and the 10th was triggered, like the classic ax that falls —to use a tremendous but very accurate image—, the Viet offensive.

The 800 Hmong, some almost children, eight or nine years old was old enough to be a good soldier, fought as always with a desperate and very lethal valor. The few Thai military did as well. No one flinched, but the barrage of .88 mortar shells and Russian Zis cannons, dragged along the jungle paths by pure strength of arms and legs, rained like a summer storm.

The American Air Force, which didn't want to involve more men than were strictly necessary in what was already beginning to take the form of a hecatomb, sent A-4 Skyhawk fighters from the aircraft carriers patrolling the Gulf of Tonkin, to machine-gun and attack with rockets and cannons the elusive soldiers of the Viet forces. But the jungle is treacherous even for what comes through the air, and in the morning on the 10th, one of those planes was shot down —it was flying almost level with the treetops and the belly was within range of the fusillade— which exploded, with all its still unused ammunition, falling between the trees and burning sixty or seventy meters around the forest, and the pilot, whose body, or what remained of it was recovered many years later, when the ups and downs of the market economy reestablished the friendship between the Indochinese and the Americans.

The Agency could be accused of being clumsy in the collection of timely information, but not of cowardice, and here it was in it as far as it could in the rescue of its people and the officers and technicians of the Air Force locked in that exit-less trap.

Air America's Bell helicopters —it seemed like a joke that a commercial airline was putting its executive machines into the boilers of hell— they were suspended two meters above the ground, avoiding as far as possible the fusillade and mortar fire, to extract from that nightmarish place what or whoever it could, alive or dead.

On the 10th in the evening, Viet climbers were already peeking out at the bare mountaintop. The explosive traps that had been placed by the defenders they deactivated, if they were recognized, or were blown by them, thus clearing the vertical path for those that came behind.

The night shone with explosions and the interrupted outline, like lines in the air, of tracer bullets.

When the ammunition ran out the Hmong took out their sharp knives and went to fetch projectiles wherever they were, in the cartridge belts and the Viet bodies, but these weren't disabled and the number and very superior firepower prevailed.

In the morning of the 11th, the pilot of a helicopter, evidently a madman, played everything to his unlikely luck and took directly from the remains of the destroyed TACAN or its surroundings the corpse of Etchberger, who died shooting (it is said that he perished in the helicopter but the versions are contradictory), and an unconscious and almost bloodless Herman Markis.

As the helicopter moved away from the stony ground and topped the summit in an evasive spiral, a 30-gauge machine gun shell hit Herman, again, in the back, and another blast killed a crewman trying to stand and knocked down the gunner from the door who fell, like a smooth stone, without shouting, into the jungle.

When they lowered him from the steaming and full of holes machine into a Long Tieng's glade —they feared that the flying ruin which was leaking oil and fuel from all sides would explode at any moment— they placed Herman on the ground, next to Etchberger's body, thinking that he had died long ago. It was a nurse that realized he was still moving and shouted for him to be carried to the infirmary.

Of the men huddled in that last helicopter, only three or four survived, although with daunting wounds, including the pilot, with several perforations in the body and multiple shrapnel and glass embedded in the eyes and skin.

Some Thai soldiers were able to escape through the jungle in the wilderness, and about thirty or forty Hmong too, although very few arrived living to their lands.

If someone was alive nothing could be done for him, only avoid the horror of becoming a prisoner of the Viet, if possible.

At dusk that same day, a Skyhawk's Captain bent over the peeled top of the Phou Pha Thi, focused his sights, gently corrected course, simultaneously pressed the release buttons of the safety pins and in a perfect launch, two, hit the middle of it with a pair of 500-pound bombs.

The deflagrations volatilized what little remained of the TACAN, the unused radio control, the remains of the last defenders and some attackers, and five or six Viet officers tracking the debris for papers, codes or anything else that might be useful to the North Vietnamese intelligence.

When the fighter-bomber, lightened of its cargo was lost on the horizon, flying eastward, back to its home, its ship, there was a thick and frightful silence on that peak now peeled to the bone. It would seem that man had never trodden that desolate place since the very first day of creation.

The Viet, who never said how many men they had lost in that brutal fight, buried their dead and returned to their starting bases.

The *phi* didn't discriminate, the sacred mountain chastised them all, without meditation or benevolence.

And many *phi* would arise from broken bodies that won't reincarnate or take centuries to do so.

But at Phou Pha Thi peace reigned again.

Somewhat gloomy, but peace in the end.

Solemn, quiet.

Stiff.

11

HONOLULU, 1968

No matter where you are in the vibrant city of Honolulu, that eclectic city near the pier and docks of Pearl Harbor to its left flank, and to its right, the famous Waikiki beach, surfing paradise and of beautiful and not so beautiful bikini girls.

If you look west you will see in the distance, on a soft wooded hill of the district of Moanalua, the splendid coral pink colored building, with the curious shape of a man, or a robot, that comes to narrow us between its enormous arms. A kind of immense very closed gothic letter C if we contemplate it from the air.

That construction, rather large in size, is the Tripler Army Medical Center, one of the largest and most important military hospitals in the United States, not only in the Pacific but in all its locations in foreign territory, which are many, and also in all of the continental country.

Within this labyrinth of hospitalization pavilions, officers VIP rooms, operating rooms, X-ray rooms, laboratories, cafeterias, kitchens, teaching rooms, offices, large spaces for physiotherapy and gymnastics, administrative offices, laundries, living quarters and *training* nurses, warehouses, garages and many other facilities was the battered body, and also the mind, very muddy still, of course, of Herman Markis, a man so disfigured that they gave him up for dead more than once, but, in spite of everything clinging to life.

After the lucky rescue at Lima Site 85, Herman Markis was stabilized as much as possible in his state of extreme gravity by a couple of nurses from the Agency base in Long Tieng and quickly transported by helicopter to a hospital of the Royal Thai army near Chiang Mai, in the north of Thailand.

"This one won't live, so don't rush!", said the pilot of the helicopter, an American who believed he had seen everything in that invisible war when he helped to lower the stretcher that was carrying an agonizing Herman.

In Chiang Mai he had a tracheostomy, was put a pair of rubber respirators on his thorax to extract the air and secretions that compressed his perforated lungs, administered blood, plasma and liquids through his veins in large quantities, was placed a tube of latex in the bladder and another one in the stomach so that he didn't drown himself in his own vomit, they splinted the legs, they bandaged him —he looked like an Egyptian mummy— and they sent him —back to the air— to Bangkok, where they surgically intervened him three times in three days and then a fourth time a week later, removing some parts of his internal organs, suturing others and withdrawing from his body, to the astonishment of the profane, not of the military surgeons accustomed to this, a whole collection of materials: crushed lead, grenade shrapnel, wood chips, shards of shells, a screw head, pebbles, buttons, cloth scraps and who knows what else.

Either he was an extremely tough guy —*un caballo*, as Cubans say— or he was very lucky, or both.

Herman didn't recall almost anything coherent about those bloody March couple of days that he spent over the top of Mount Phou Pha Thi. Everything was represented in his haunted head like a nebulous, dark and dazzling whirlwind, but he remembered even less the weeks in which he was floating at the edges of death.

"Fragile life was pulling him by one arm and Lady Death by the other", a very scrupulous Thai practitioner, who practiced Buddhism, explained.

He had an imprecise idea of an already very pregnant Ana who laid on the bed and pressed his left hand —the right was mutilated and splinted— to the sweet smell of halothane, an anesthetic that deepened his unconsciousness every time they opened him to sew or extract something, and from many faces that came near to mumble things he didn't understand or forgot almost immediately.

Approximately a month and a half later he was transferred —for the first time not in a helicopter— in a Hercules C-130 transport airplane belonging to the medical wing of the Air Force. They made, Herman wasn't even aware of it, two intermediate stops in Saigon and Manila, to finally arrive at the Honolulu airport and from there by ambulance to Tripler Hospital.

Ana, six months and a half pregnant, joined him, with her heart in her mouth and death in her soul, in a couple of days. Although they had to operate Herman again to extract a piece of forgotten shrapnel inside one of his thighs, which already reeked through the hole of a suppurating fistula, he now felt fully aware and with a few pains, to say something, and he didn't wish this even to the mothers of those damn Viet.

As the weeks went by, Herman learned, in bits and pieces, of some good and some very bad things: Ana's pregnancy was going well and that Herman Rub, their son, was in the care of Suyin and Dr. Sirikit in Bangkok, that Etch and the other officers who fought alongside him on that damn mountain were all dead, that the Hmong, his faithful warriors, had been practically annihilated and the most unpleasant and ugly of all, which came from the lips of a USAF Colonel and an Agency officer who visited him together one afternoon in which they kindly sent all those that were in the room out:

"Herman, you and your companions are, without a doubt, heroes, and deserve the highest decorations", said the Colonel.

Herman thanked him with his head but without opening his mouth.

"And all of you will be granted, of course, medals, —he continued—, but for now and for everyone, including your families, everyone has died and you have been badly injured in a helicopter crash in Thailand".

None of them could have known in that aseptic hospital room, but the honorary Medal of Honor of the Armed Forces rightly assigned to Chief Master Sergeant Richard Etchberger was given to his sons, mature men, on September 21st, 2010 by President Obama, forty-two and a half years behind schedule, but that is another issue that's not relevant to this chronicle.

Herman assimilated that, no questions asked and without looking at the faces of the two men, who stood almost in attention, very close together, anxious to get out of there.

"Do you understand us clearly?", asked the civilian.

As he gazed up at the ceiling, Herman spoke in a very low voice, with the difficulty that a deep wound in his chin that had not yet healed completely caused, and a little because of the disgust that rose up his stomach.

"I understand, sir", he sounded sour and mocking.

"Great", said the other guy without much enthusiasm.

"And the Hmong?", Herman's voice was cavernous.

"We will try to help the families of these men, but don't worry about that now". —One of them, the one in the gray suit, covered his mouth and coughed—. "Think about your recovery, Markis, the war's already behind you".

"You need to rest", said the one in uniform.

Herman, unexpectedly, rang the emergency bell with the small white switch within reach of his left hand.

"Let me rest in peace then". —A flash of the mulatto of his nightmares sprang to his mind, spitting at the execution squad and himself—. "Please". —He turned his head to the other side—. "Fuck off, will you?"

"Don't take it so hard Herman, we know you feel bad and..."

"Bullshit!" —he coughed and seemed to choke—. "*¡No me lo tomo de ninguna cabrona manera, coño!*", this he said in Spanish. "Go to hell already!"

The colonel looked at the other and nodded at the door.

"Don't get angry Herman, but remember, what we have told you is an order from the higher ups and..."

The colonel interrupted the man in the overcoat and touched Herman's arm rather gently, as if broken, perhaps as a gesture of friendly farewell.

"Don't forget, Herman, don't forget, it is not our decision, so you have to follow it, please".

"I won't forget, sir, but get out of here and fuck off, get out of my sight before I start asking for help, will you!"

A nurse with yellow hair and a sharp face, topped by a white bonnet, opened the door of the room and looked inside:

"Is something wrong, gentlemen?"

The Agency man turned and reassured her:

"It's all right miss, we're leaving".

"Fucking good!", Herman grunted.

"Goodbye, Herman, rest and remember that we need you back on the ground".

"Yes gentlemen, I will rest when you two and those who sent you, those sons of bitches, go to fucking hell!"

The two men evaporated in silence without saying goodbye.

Herman refused to eat that afternoon, slept badly, needed more painkillers than usual, and didn't say a word to Ana or anyone until the next morning.

Then, when the day was breaking, after a night of insomnia and suffering, he said his first word, or rather, three:

"Sons of bitches!"

12

BANGKOK, 1972

Now they were four.

The boy, a cheerful and sturdy blend of blond-haired Cuban-American with a Thai accent, had just turned seven. The new baby who was about to be four years old, was a brunette like her mother and somewhat quieter and calmer than Rub, with a temper like her Aunt Gretel, an aunt lost in the distance that Ana didn't stop remembering and mention very often.

Ana María had been promoted to mathematics and geometry teacher in the American School, where she was popular and had become a kind of mentor: fashion, parental problems, correspondent and unrequited love, soft sex mess-ups —the hard ones were yet to come—, embarrassments... in short, a counselor for everything of a group of adolescent teens from other lands and cultures that they often longed for.

Just like she did so often.

Suyin had also risen to be a housekeeper —without stopping buying fresh food every day from the boats anchored in the canals and cooking, of course, that she didn't delegate—, but now with the help of a niece of indeterminate age that she had brought from her hometown, eighteen or twenty years old, difficult to know her real age, who took care of all the other tasks in the house, and did it very well, by the way.

Everyone was doing well, except Herman.

Although with obvious mutilations, the left leg slightly shorter than the other, three fingers less in his right hand, a whole mural of scars —he even joked that he had as many seams as a baseball— in his abdomen, chest, back, limbs and lower jaw, physical health was not what most mortified him.

It was his head.

He tried to explain to himself over and over what had happened at Phou Pha Thi. "Why had the enemy been underestimated? Why I wasn't able to prevent that disaster? Why? Why?"

An opponent who had been able to develop, defend and maintain, even against the massive bombardments of the B-52s and F-111s, a supply line that started from the border of North Vietnam, crossed a good part of Laos and Cambodia to finish digging like the roots of a healthy tree in Southern Vietnam.

"How could he not alert his bosses with enough time and energy? Why was he alive?"

He was glad of being alive, still savoring a cold beer, or several; he loved his wife and his children, he enjoyed them, well, relatively. But he imagined her disgusted by his large scars and the repulsive marks on his body, although Ana denied it and gave herself to him more or less as before, but...

"Why the fuck had he survived that mess?

Why were they all buried, or worse, lost in the jungle, but him?"

He slept little, or slept soundly when the sun was already break-ing, and then, having to rise at dawn, he would crawl all morning like an old sick man, until he discovered that a vodka, or two, and sometimes three lifted him up with encouragement and an improved mood.

He still had nightmares about the mulatto and his spit, but now a new hallucination had been added to it —a memory he couldn't have, for he was unconscious and almost dead as everyone pointed out— with Etch's bleeding body convulsing and vomiting blood and phlegm above his belly as they both clung to each other so as not to fall through the open door of that damned helicopter that gave desperate strokes from one side to the other trying to avoid what was almost inevitable.

He could describe in detail the chaos and piling up of shattered bodies inside the cockpit of that machine, moving disorderly and always about to fall to the ground, but no, the psychiatrists, the few friends, Ana, had convinced him —a figure of speech— that this was impossible, although this was the way this unthinkable flight had been, more or less.

"It's just that the logic of what had to have happened has gotten into your head as if you had really seen it", they told him, but... "wise words, but fuck, I really think I saw it!"

However, of the battle at that ridge, in which he did fight with full consciousness, he could remember almost nothing. Some cries, isolated orders, imprecations and detonations in clusters, clotted blood, shrieks of the Viet, someone crying and asking for his mother to protect him from Hell. What did his brain do with the 48 hours he was fighting on the summit of that bitch mountain?

He couldn't remember, however much he tried, the face of Etch, or the features of the commander who had traveled with him towards death.

The headaches didn't torment him as much as his back, but they fucked him up, and he preferred not to take painkillers, although sometimes, when the torture was too much, he surrendered.

He was dizzy and his heart was racing when he was frightened by something he couldn't control —not only when he went overboard with his vodka or beers— but that he could control, unless Ana or the children were the cause, like the dreadful day in the time of the monsoon in which they were surprised in the street by a deluge with lightning and thunder that seemed it would destroy everything.

She came soaked, her hair undone and her clothes drenched, but happy. Rub in Ana's hand and the girl in her arms, but all cheerful and telling the odyssey that had just happened in the flooded streets, and that they wouldn't eat something hot that night because the electricity was out in almost all the city thrown in.

And he was almost killed by anxiety and fear.

The first psychiatrist he spoke to at Tripler Hospital in Honolulu, a young, pleasant man with a New England accent and gestures, showed him, quite logically, the foolishness of his guilty thoughts.

"You couldn't Herman, in any way, have foreseen that attack. Your job was training and preparation for defense, but you didn't handle intelligence information". —The man looked into his eyes and there was truth in his words—. "It was the duty of other bastards who meanwhile were daydreaming and eating their buggers. Have you thought about that?" —He stared into his eyes with a clear, transparent look—. "Did you know?"

The doctor was a nice and very convincing guy, very professional but with his feet well on the ground.

"It was the Air Force suckers who thought the Viet were stupid assholes, well, they weren't!"

He put a warm hand on his knee.

"You were put on that mountain, together with your comrades, to defend their shit radar". —He let a few seconds pass—. You followed an order, and in what way, but they didn't back you up, Herman.

He shook his head, showing his rage.

"They gave the Hmong the task instead of sending a battalion of rangers, or two, or three, or whatever they needed, the 82nd airborne in full, to fight the whole damn army of fucking Uncle Ho!" —He punched the office table—. "Oh, so the world wouldn't know!" —He walked over to a cooler and pulled out two cans of Coke.

He offered one to Herman.

"Take it, it's a good head medicine".

Herman was staring at him, dumbfounded.

"Take away those regrets, with no reason, from your fucking head at once, Herman!"

He established a good relationship with that shrink —who had the balls to tell him that he shouldn't tell anyone that he knew that this tragedy had been a full-fledged battle and not a helicopter accident, as it was written on the medical chart— and he felt much better, even without medicines, but unfortunately he stopped seeing him when he returned to Thailand.

He was back in Honolulu a few months later for another surgical procedure that allowed him to finally get out of the wheelchair. But his favorite shrink had gone to civil practice, as his nurse friends told him, in an elegant office for depressed ladies by the excessive weight of jewelry and important impotent gentlemen, near Rodeo Drive, in fucking California! Obviously a very clever fellow, that damn shrink.

With the military psychiatrists in Bangkok all he did was waste time: Take this three times a day, don't take this but that, don't take anything, rest, try to sleep, one pill every four hours, count sheep if you can't sleep, don't drink, one tablet every twelve hours, eat healthy, walk, don't think, anybody has an accident... And so, session after session, consultation after consultation.

They looked a lot like the Colonel and the guy from the Agency who had once visited him in the Tripler room.

"Let them also go to hell, and fuck off!"

Getting back to work, now as an intelligence analyst who obtained on the ground anti-communist rebels, almost all Hmong who crossed the Mekong River, constantly, between Laos and northern Thailand, did him well.

Boy, it did him good!

He left the house, breathed the air. Sometimes he even traveled to Chiang Mai on airplanes from the Thai or North American Air Force —which made his palms sweat, his armpits, his forehead beaded with drops of perspiration, his belly writhing of fear, he always had an urge to pee, he choked, his mouth felt like sandpaper, and all that he learned to hide like an expert— when the information was oral and important. He related to people to some extent and felt useful, and above all, he had the perception, which relieved him, that he was freeing Ana and the children from his dark presence.

He loved them very, very much, but he preferred not to be near them.

He didn't like being seen.

He clung to work with a certain obsession, first, and then with an absolute surrendering, bordering sometimes on nonsense, according to his companions.

Even the Thai wondered what happened to that guy who screwed around so much. He was stubbornly clung to the cause, lost beforehand, of the Hmong. And he also clung, when he had a space, however small, to the bottle.

Loyal friend, the bottle. Loyal and fitting.

Discreet.

13

Don Muang Airport, 1973

The new year brought, revealing how relentless the passing of existence is, the ten-year anniversary of the escape from Cuba, a purely personal celebration that had transformed their lives forever.

"Ten years? My God, who would say?", Ana said very quietly as she stroked Herman's hair one Sunday morning in one of those rare good weeks that he had, especially when they had made love slowly, with the lights off, under the sheets and without many gymnastic and bodily demands.

"How many things have happened, and also two children who at any moment are out of our hands?, Herman replied.

"There's still a lot of time left for that, Herman, don't be so American".

"I'm a gringo, and you too, *ricura caribeña*".

She kissed him on the mouth, tongue and all, with a fresh passion that no longer showed up as often as before.

The new year also brought splendid news, another miracle for Ana María: A black American Pastor, an African-American politician, as one might say, precisely one of the strongest opponents of the Indochina war, had visited Castro in Havana on occasion of some national festivities and had brought with him, as a kind of gift of goodwill to the gringo radical left, several political prisoners from the Cuban prisons accompanied by their closest relatives.

And among them was her brother Máximo, her mother and her sister Gretel, who were tried by the US Immigration Department as political asylees and provisionally housed in Miami, in the home of a relative of the late Rubino.

Ana María immediately phoned Gretel —the sobs and years of not hearing each other almost didn't allow them to understand each other— and when she hung up she quickly began to prepare the long trip from Bangkok to Miami to meet them, just after ten years of not seeing them, and in the case of Máximo, almost twelve.

Ana was able to make it clear that everyone was in good health, including Máximo, who had been taken at dawn from a huge prison built during another dictatorship, that of General Gerardo Machado, located on an island south of the Province of Havana, brought up, without explaining, to a military plane that flew to the Havana airport and there boarded again on the rented aircraft that brought the Pastor and his entourage, without seeing anyone or anything. From jail to Miami without looking to the sides, with blinkers like horses, as Gretel ironically put it.

"But is he healthy, *mi hermana*?"

"Oh, yes, quite healthy in this case, Ana María. We, the Santana Donremí have an armored heart".

Ana Donremí floated in the happiness of recovering her son but it wasn't easy to detach her from that probable tomb to which she was still tied. Gretel explained to Ana that she had been promised, at some time in the near future, to exhume the remains and bring them into exile, but that this had been nothing more than a pretext to get her on the plane.

In short, Máximo's care, to get him back under her skirt, was what convinced her, and if she hadn't found him inside the plane —a heartbreaking scene for both of them, as they later told Ana María— she would have turned her back right there, and it probably would have been forever.

And Gretel? Well, they would talk until they were tired of it.

Herman found out a few days later —he was in the highlands classifying documents captured from the Viet somewhere near the Ho Chi Minh route, by a ghost squad of Hmong rebels— and returned as soon as he could to hug Ana and see their children before departing.

Ana María probed the possibility of him going with them.

Herman was emphatic:

"Ana María, you know that I love you so and that your happiness is my best gift, but I won't go with you to Miami in any way". —He looked into her eyes with a tenderness that was already becoming unknown between them—. "You have a debt with your mother and it's time to pay it off".

She took his hands with unusual force:

"Come with us, the past is the past and you are not to blame for anything that may have happened to my family". —Tears streamed down her shining face.

"I told you one day that we would see what I could do for your family and I couldn't do anything". He cried like that afternoon in the warm, blue water of Guanabo Beach.

"Now you can do much for them, and I will support you in everything, but as for me, this, for now, is my place on Earth, it is my war, Ana, and however we do in it, it's not finished yet".

Ana didn't extend too much or put too much emphasis on the controversy. In the end, Ana María was relieved that Herman wouldn't met with her family, whom he had hardly knew —he had only seen Gretel on the evening of the wedding, and sometime again—, on this first occasion.

There would be time to prepare the ground for a friendly meeting, considering that he, Herman, was on the same side of the late Rubino and was the father of Ana Donremí's only two grandchildren.

When Rub and Greta —Gretel María the girl was called— would secure, with the candor and the intelligence with which they knew how to move in the world of adults (Ana suspected that Suyin and her Buddhism had something to do with the way of being and behaving of her children), the relationship with Máximo and especially with the grandmother, would open the way for Herman to be accepted unconditionally in the family.

She, who asked the Virgin in her prayers, was sure, well, almost certain, that in the end she would succeed, and perhaps they would be very happy and eat partridges, like in the stories.

The Agency —these were other times— provided them with round-trip tickets, almost free of charge, at Pan American, and included Suyin on the travelers list, with a tourist visa, without a prior written request, in a couple of days.

They lived in a contradictory time; on the one hand, people were killed with a medieval savagery, without pity or care, as the Viet did with their enemies, piercing them with bamboo spikes or destroying them with string bombs. Or like the B-52 pilots reciprocated with everything underneath, carpeted the ground with magnesium bombs until the heat melted the earth and made it shine at night. But at the same time, the forms, the formal rules, were kept, in short, it was a world of crazies framed in rules of formal education and urban behavior.

In just over a week —luggage, Ana's paid leave at the American School, money for the trip, and reservations to accommodate the newcomers in Miami, plane tickets, Suyin's family farewells and other trivialities that never ceased to be indispensable— they were ready to leave.

The happier of the lot was, without a doubt, Ana; the most excited about adventure and the unknown was Rub; the more calm, Greta; and Suyin was fright made flesh, but sieved by the acceptance of the inevitable befitting of Thais.

Herman said his farewells with a hug and a few recommendations for the long flight in the VIP lounge of Don Muang Airport. He waited quietly behind the greenish glass of the upper terrace of the air terminal until PANAM's Boeing 707-320 was lost in the gray, but not intimidating, clouds that bordered the horizon.

Very rarely Herman communicated with God, or with the good *phi*, but this time he did it to ask for a smooth journey for the only ones he really cared in the world, the only ones he had, except for a few Hmong with whom he had established a strange relationship of comradeship and mutual admiration —they didn't forget Phou Pha Thi and other equally or more bloody events that weren't to be divulged—, which was based on the diaphanous character of their positions: while you are with me, I am with you, truly and to the end, if you are not with me... if you are not with me then you'll know what to expect.

It was raining lightly, Thank God! When he left the sprawling Don Muang parking lot and drove to the outskirts of Bangkok. He drove his '68 Chevrolet Corvair —it was old but he liked it— along the hellish truck traffic with impossible loads, bicycles, shabby jeeps, cars that miraculously worked, few luxurious high-end black cars, rickshaws, buses crowded up to the roof, trucks, scooters, pedestrians with huge bundles in their backs, the chaos, until arriving to the solitary apartment.

He climbed alone in the elevator, opened the door to his house, got off his clothes and his personal weapon and settled on the terrace, before loading a glass and a bucket with ice.

He unscrewed the lid of a new bottle of legitimate Stolichnaya vodka, the good liquor of the enemy, from the unfathomable Thai black market.

He dropped five or six ice cubes into the glass and poured a generous stream of the drink —man, such good alcohol the Russians made!— until he filled it.

If something the Russians have done well, to be honest, in addition to their immortal novels, that's the Stolichnaya vodka and the AK-47 rifle, two of the most appreciated goods by the North Americans who had to survive boredom and death in the Indochina of those dangerous years.

He took a long, relaxing sip, and set his feet on a stool.

He had all the time in the world to think in peace.

All the time.

14

Chiang Mai, 1973

When one least expects it, the sun comes out. Ana María's meeting with her mother, Ana Donremí, so feared by her, was serene, harmonious, even cordial.

Ana Donremí didn't make comments or scenes about what had happened twelve or thirteen years earlier, as if they had normally saw each other a month ago. She hugged and kissed her daughter, wrapped the two children together in her arms and said affectionate things that they could hardly understand but recognized as good and friendly, and to everyone's surprise also took Suyin's hands and thanked her for what she was doing for her daughter and her grandchildren.

"You are a very noble and good chinita". —She took from her purse a holy card of the Virgen de La Caridad del Cobre, kissed it with unction and gave it to the Thai woman—. "I can't repay you enough for how good you are with them and how beautiful you dress them, how well you feed them and how much you care about their well-being". —And a single tear ran down her face.

Suyin at first looked Ana, who was also expectant and confused, but the little Thai, with the Asians' natural spark, swiftly recovered, kissed the little effigy with respect and tucked it under her blouse, between her breasts.

"They all good with me, missus". —Quickly, she reached into her duffel bag and placed a tiny Hirunyak imitation mask in Ana Donremí's hand, a small figure of small commercial value but delicately crafted and very beautiful.

"Thank you my little girl, I will always keep it as a memory of you". —And put it between her fleshy and broad breasts.

"Thank to you, missus".

The two women, apparently so different, didn't cease to have everyone open-mouthed with stupor.

If it wasn't a mutual feeling of goodwill, which seemed so, that meeting was a lesson of high diplomacy.

Then Ana Donremí stepped aside, scratched her right eye, smiled with acquiescence and let the brothers roam free again. She had fulfilled her part beyond expectations, in that elegant way, much to her old, stale, grand lady's style, and decided that it was time to return to her usual reserve.

The ghost of Herman, who was in many ways in the minds of everyone, was not a character in that drama.

Máximo had become an old man long before he was forty: he spoke little, he was hunched over, his teeth were a mess, his hands shaked, his hairline had become a baldness of thin tufts, he had hemorrhoids and a persistent urticaria on his neck, armpits and forearms, he slept poorly, he ate without appetite, it constantly came to his memory his fellow inmates.

"How are they doing, would they have visitors, would they have eaten, poor boys, were the fierce requisitions that the guards make in their cells, when they feel like it, very hard?"

And he had no idea how an automatic transmission car was driven, how a dishwasher was used, a cordless telephone, how the TV channels were switched with the remote control or a bank account was opened.

A tormented soul, a shadow of the bright, jovial and somewhat crazy athlete, irresistible to the girls around him of what had been a different time.

In a way, as he later explained to Ana María and Gretel a Cuban doctor from the shelter who thoroughly reviewed Máximo and talked for a long time with him more in a friendly manner than professionally, Máximo had become institutionalized.

"Institutionalized. What does that mean, doctor?", Ana María asked with her mouth open.

That meant, and it was a horror, that when he entered prison so young and spent so many years in it, his psyche had adapted to prison life.

"Look, ladies, what I'm going to say may seem like nonsense, but this is in medical books and we see it frequently here". —He tapped the palm of his left hand with his stethoscope while he was seated on the edge of the desk—. Your brother 'misses' life in prison, it is as if he has a hard time living outside bars. —He shook his head from side to side as if he himself thought it impossible—. In prison, the risks are known, and most of the prisoners end up dominating them, but life in freedom is something else, scary. —He stopped and headed for the office door—. But with time it'll pass.

"My God!"

"You think so, Doctor?"

"It will pass, he's still very young, luckily for him, and it'll pass". —He shook hands and gestured the exit for them—. You'll remember me when that happens, you'll see.

To settle Máximo's limitations and calamities was a question of time, over the course of months, as the doctor had predicted, and of the determination and the patience that the family he had recovered should have.

Ana María's meeting with Gretel was different.

The sisters had so much to say that they understood that at dawn, when everyone slept and nothing and no one bothered them —telephone calls of old acquaintances, they didn't have any friends per se, untimely visits, the search for a house to live in, the paperwork, immigration, shopping, having almost nothing to wear, childcare, peremptory efforts and everything else—, would be their hours of catching up, sharing confidences, trying to appropriate with words of everything lived and suffered during those heartbreaking years that now seemed like a sigh.

Herman, for his part, after taking advantage of his stay in Bangkok to put in order all documents related to his status within the Agency, salaries and premiums accrued and to be accrued, bonuses for decorations (all secret) and injuries in war or covert operations, clarify the compensation he would receive in case of retirement or his wife in case he died on active duty —he was reminded of a bureaucrat, and couldn't avoid a certain mockery in his comment that he had almost died in 'a helicopter crash' during a routine service—, and even in the hypothetical case of being MIA (missing in action), a possibility that made the same official laugh:

"Sir, it is much better that the body, whatever remains of the corpse, you know, the pieces, appear because if they don't it becomes a tremendous mess for your family to collect the little pension".

The guy, a shorty surely a son or grandson of chicanos, thought himself a comedian.

"Without a dog-tag with your name, sir, I think they have to wait like five years to see a dollar, so pray for the dog-tag to turn up even if you are turned into a burned and unrecognizable pulp".

"Oh, yeah?"

"What's left is not as important as the tag". —He gestured with a certain pleasure the one that hung around his neck—. "Don't forget, sir, that little tag with your name and identification number is your-self, it is much more valuable than the bones that the worms leave cleaned, ok, Holmes?"

How much it pissed Herman to be talked to in diminutives!

But the Holmes was right, he'd heard those stories before, and this bastard knew the whole thing firsthand, not because he'd seen actual death at all, but because he'd processed the papers of the deceased, which apparently that was what had value.

"Thanks for the information, Holmes!"

The guy almost pisses himself of laughter.

After the arrangements were made, which he should have done a long time ago, and put everything in order, he managed to talk for a long time on the telephone with Ana María, calculating the time difference and avoiding frequent interruptions due to static or lim-itations of the communication lines on the Asian side.

He was glad of the absence of problems with his mother-in-law, whom he didn't know personally, but had seen in old photos.

He chose not to talk to the children:

"I'll talk to them later, I'm satisfied with knowing that they're well and enjoying Miami, they already deserved a trip like that!"

Ana María sounded safe and calm, satisfied that everything was going better than expected.

"I'm straightening things up here to get back to you as soon as possible". —He felt her hesitate—. "You don't know how much I want to go back to our house".

"How has Suyin been in Miami?"

"You have no idea how she has adapted, and she even has my mother in her pocket, which is a lot to say, that chinawoman is a treasure, Herman!"

"She's Thai, Ana, she's not Chinese".

"I know, chico, it's a matter of speech!"

"You've been in Miami for fifteen days and you're already talking like a Cuban, Ana!"

"Shit, as if you're American!"

For a moment they were like before, laughing eagerly, happy, even blissful.

Right time to say their goodbyes.

That night Herman drank little and slept early, without nightmares, without the company of the dead, as he hadn't done for a long time.

At dawn, fortunately it didn't rain, he went to the airport and returned, without any fuss or apprehension, on a Thai transport plane —one of those unavoidable World War II equipment— to the Agency facilities in Chiang Mai.

From Chiang Mai Herman was now waging his war, a struggle that he knew to be lost, like those defeated marching to the execution wall of the old fortress there on the island, who died ignoring that, as time passed, years, the victors of the moment would slowly descend, or in flash —like the man in the black beret, of which his little bones were weaved in some lost jungle in Bolivia— towards rot, the accommodation and the abandonment of ideals.

"Ideals? What the fuck did that even mean?" —A shitty illusion that had pushed them to become criminals.

"And also victims".

"Was there such a difference?"

It didn't matter. Herman had already secured his rearguard.

Then, without encumbrance and without bundles, back, happy, to the battle, closer to his aggressive Hmong and his dead.

And away from his remorse.

Far away.

15

MEKONG RIVER, 1973

The Laotian Hmong rebels, saving their physical and idiomatic differences, reminded Herman of the rough Cuban peasants in the mountainous areas known as the Escambray mountain ranges, located in the center of the island of Cuba. *Guajiros* —that's how people called the peasants in Cuba— who had risen in arms against the Castro government almost from the very beginning of his regime. Not accepting, except for very few exceptions, lands, benefits and compensations for having fought also, from their dense and isolated hills, against the dictatorship of Fulgencio Batista.

In fact, a portion of those harsh *guajiros* had been soldiers and officers of the same rebel army, now reinforced by thousands and thousands of militiamen, who were confronted with the almost suicidal courage of those who didn't have much to lose.

A bunch of systematic oppositionist fools, as they were sometimes called, by the man in the black beret.

A hard, very hard nut to crack, seemingly immune to physical exertion, hunger and pain, incredibly skillful to fool the enemy and an extreme and refined cruelty to make him suffer, attached to their land, resigned to early death, simulators, cunning, sly but brave until bordering on insanity and faithful to their faithful... and nothing more than their tried and true faithful, and if they were linked by blood ties, even better.

It was not uncommon for those families settled in the mountains to have ten or twelve dead in combat or executed among their members: parents, children, siblings, uncles, nephews, but anyways, this is war, they told you with no regret, and off to something else.

In his time in the fortress, Herman had had very little to do with the tragic end of these men who carried the nickname bandits, for most of them died fighting or were shot —after mock trials that could last, with favorable time, between five and fifteen minutes— in the same places where they were captured or in the grounds of areas owned by the Army if it was considered worth interrogating them, which used to end in a waste of time and in a barrage of insults and insolence for the improvised, or not so much, investigators and prosecutors of the State Security.

And so, although a little more surly and reserved, much less expressive and more refinedly cruel, of course, more Asian, were the Hmong.

It hadn't been easy for the Agency to ingratiate itself with these natural rebels, but being the enemies of their mortal enemies, the Viet, the free flow of arms, ammunition and supplies (the Hmong cultivated only rice and opium) and the courageous and frank attitude of some Americans operating directly on the ground had established ties that would extend over time to well beyond the end of the war in Indochina.

Tobey Pao was a Hmong boss for whom Herman felt a particular sense of respect, admiration, rather, and in turn, especially after Phou Pha Thi, that consideration was rewarded by him, allowing him an access to his environment that wasn't granted almost to no one, let alone a foreigner, a target.

Once the Kingdom of Thailand decided to officially and publicly withdraw its military aid to the government of South Vietnam, and already in the process of Vietnamisation, that hypocritical political word, that the government of Nixon and Mr. Kissinger invented to cover up the shameful escape of that senseless slaughter, Laos was literally in the hands of the army of North Vietnam and its national allies, the Pathet Lao.

And of course the Hmong, the unshakable friends of the Americans, the red-blooded anticommunists, were left to their (bad) luck.

To their shuddering and deleterious bad luck.

Even the Agency's more or less covert operations within the territory of Laos were being dismantled and many of its special mission officers in the field transferred to other destinations or retired. Something that would happen, in a very short time, to maintain the same policy and didn't see a compelling reason to change it, with Herman himself, who by the way, had a collection of scars, both in body and brain, enough to take refuge, far, back in his land, to the peaceful life of the pensioner.

The Hmong, decimated to the point that they had almost no combatants who were over twelve or thirteen years old, and forcefully torn away from their meager rice paddies and from the increasingly meager profits offered by opium, from which they vitally depended to survive, were taking refuge in the plateaus and forests of northern Thailand. Many of them, or their diminished descendants, would return over the years, more than a quarter of a century later, to a Laos with a kinder government or would end up as refugees in the West Coast of North America. But at that moment the Hmong had only two choices: either they would retreat, leaving behind a crop of corpses, to the abrupt mountainous area of Phou Bia, the highest and most inaccessible of the central ridge —9,000 feet high or more— a sort of cemetery of elephants lost among the clouds, or fled to Thailand to survive and wait.

With that dark panorama ahead, Herman found himself, once again, with Tobey Pao. They found each other in a glade near the village of Chiang Khong (later, that tiny village would grow to be a pretentious tourist town from which the Mekong Tour would begin, including, of course, Laos), about eight hours away from Chiang Mai, by jeep, by infernal clay and chalk roads, right on the Thai Mekong River, the great river, the river of rivers for the Indochinese.

Herman Markis came alone and unarmed to the place they both knew from previous secret encounters. Pao, also disarmed, was accompanied by some silent companions, all very similar to him, carrying their AR–15's and AK–47's, and most probably by others, well hidden in the jungle, that would not let be seen by anyone.

They greeted each other with consideration and appreciation, very much like Hmong's do.

"Did everything go well across the river, Tobey?", Herman asked with calculated deference.

"Very well, Mr. Herman, the river is a friend, it's not our problem, our misfortunes come from there, He pointed east toward Vietnam.

A companion of Pao, perhaps one of his sons and obviously fierce bodyguard, a fox with sharp fangs, carefully placed the rifle on a dry trunk and began to prepare a tea of aromatic leaves, so boiling that Herman had to blow —Pao mockingly teased the weaknesses of white people— so as to not burn his lips and tongue.

"Heat is life, Mr. Herman".

"Heat burns, Pao".

"Oh, yes, like napalm!" —The Hmong laughed with his horse-like laughter.

After spending a few minutes slowly drinking tea and more inconsequential talk, Tobey Pao began the tirade that had brought him to that lonely place risking his life and that of his men.

"Mr. Herman (Markis never used fictitious names with the Hmong and they knew it, and they knew how to appreciate that detail), I have not yet lived thirty years, and I'm already a venerable old man among my people". —He made an emphatic silence— almost all our men have gone, warring, to the country of the *phi*, and we only have these children here to fight against the Viet, but we continue, and we will continue fighting until the last of us says goodbye and our people remain only in memory, if someone is to bring us up in his mind.

Herman nodded, downcast.

"I know, Pao, and that's why I'm here to listen to you, and if it's in my power, to help you".

"Sir, to the Viet and their servants we are only bandits, vermin, and their intent is to crush us, or drag us towards slavery". —He looked at Herman with a cold, penetrating look that almost made him shudder—. And they will, no doubt, if fate wants us to be unarmed.

Herman took some time before answering:

"What can we do for you, Pao?"

"We have fought together for a long time, sir, but we hear rumors that you will abandon us".

"I don't know, Pao, I've never lied to you and I'm not going to now". —He sat up slowly—. "I can't discern what my government will do, but I know what I'm willing to do, which is not much, but it's something".

Tobey Pao nodded with deference.

"Defeating the Viet is impossible". —He paused and frowned for a while, which Herman respected without moving or opening his mouth—. "But it is possible to save something from my people by bringing it here, crossing the river".

Herman nodded again.

"To obtain the permit of transit and temporary stay from the Royal Thai Government is my duty Pao, count on that, you have my word".

"I expected that from you, Herman, but there's something else".

"I hear you".

"Some of us will not come, they were born there, where the sun rises". —He pointed east, across the Mekong, and toward the high cloud-covered mountains on the horizon—. "And there they will die, sir, and they will rot on the tops of the cliffs, near the birds, eaten by the birds, and their bones will whiten in the sun, that is their desire".

"That must be respected, Pao".

"And it will be". —He pointed a thin finger at Herman's chest—. "But they want to die killing, sir, like their ancestors, as it should be, so that their immortal souls may gain the peace they deserve and not become malevolent *phi*".

"They need weapons and ammunition, don't they, Pao?"

"That's right, sir".

"They'll have them, not many, but they will have them".

"What we ask for is little for what the Viet and its lackeys have".

"I know, and I can't offer you anything but rifles and bullets, Tobey".

"I trust in your word, sir, to die by killing, that's enough".

"If I have to I'll do it on my own, Pao, and as soon as possible".

Herman took two steps toward Pao and shook hands firmly in agreement, an agreement between men that was worth much more than a paper with letters on it.

"Tobey?" —the small, wiry Hmong chief bowed—. Now it's me who wants to ask something of you.

"If it is in my poor hands to do something for you, sir".

"Not for us, Tobey, for me, and forget about my government and my bosses". —He held Pao's hands even more tightly in both hands—.

"It's for me, Tobey, my friend". —He waited a few seconds before continuing—. "This is a small personal matter that must remain between you and me".

"The life of my people, and their worthy and honorable passage to the world of the dead, depends now on you, Mr. Herman". —He nodded hard to reaffirm his words—. "That's why my life is yours, sir".

Pao stared at Herman, "You can ask for it anytime".

"No, Tobey, you owe your life to your people!" —He let his hands off Pao's and gathered them, palm-to-palm, to the front of his chest.

"It's of my life that I want to talk with you!"

"Of your life, sir?"

"Yes, Tobey, of my life!"

He pointed to himself with the index of his right hand.

"Or of my death!"

16

LANGLEY, VIRGINIA, 1974

A young gentleman and an even younger lady, both slender and elegant, expensive clothes, well-dressed —Bloomingdale's, Hermes, Chanel, stuff like that— received, discreetly but with style, Ana María, next to the somewhat worn dark rubber carpet at the exit of gate B 14 at John Foster Dulles Airport in Fairfax/Loudoun, a few miles north of the Washington, DC metro area.

"Mrs. Markis?"

"Indeed".

They stepped aside to allow the free passage of hurried travelers behind her and the two shook her hand with courtesy and delicacy.

Educated gestures, Ivy League manners, class.

The TWA flight was only a few minutes late from San Francisco with a stopover at Kansas City's mid-airport in the center of the country. And Ana María felt tired and dizzy enough, after more than a full day's travel from Bangkok, plus the radical alteration of her time zones, to feel like socializing.

The laziness in her legs, the stabbing in her back and the demurred, pale face made her look ill or intoxicated, and she was drunk, but of tiredness and restlessness.

"Mrs. Markis, my partner and I think you must feel exhausted".

The girl took her by the arm and the young man asked for her travel bag to carry it on the long walk to the reception desk located on the floor below.

"We will take you to a good hotel in Arlington where you can rest from this long journey, eat a hot meal and recover".

"And you will feel like new tomorrow morning, you'll see".

They told her their names, which she thought were too common: John and Susan or something, and they walked slowly —the effort was noticeable of those two athletes to slow their pace— the long corridor of the air terminal until arriving, after descending an escalator, to the luggage conveyor belt.

Ana was carrying a single suitcase, with a mother-of-pearl handle, very fashionable at the time, not too big, and the young man also took care of it once he identified it.

When they got her —the two of them went up with her in the elevator after picking up the key and sign her in at the reception— in a pleasant room at a good Arlington hotel, Ana María was on the verge of fainting.

"Can we help you with anything else, ma'am?"

"You've done too much for me". —She smiled gratefully—. I want to wash and rest in silence, I need to sleep.

Both nodded with a smile of perfect white teeth.

"Here's our phone number". —She was given a card with a telephone number, and nothing else—. "We are at your disposal for whatever you may need".

Once in the pleasant and modern bedroom, she showered with the water as hot as possible, soaped herself several times with a scented liquid soap and aromatic salts, took a couple of aspirins and a sleeping pill with a Coke, the only thing that her stomach could endure after that succession of food and drinks with which she was crammed with in the first-class section of the airplane, and threw herself on the bed, wrapped in a huge spongy towel.

Only a small part of the immense bed she had undone, throwing aside the sky-blue bedspread that covered it.

Her thoughts, now that she was bathed and relaxed, took her back to Bangkok, a year ago, the afternoon when an official from the US embassy —he introduced himself as such— picked her up at the American School and took her, in a large black car, a Ford LTD, to a somewhat close consular office where two other persons awaited her, one of them a military man, whom after a brief greeting she begged them to get to the point.

The news were confusing, just like everything relating her husband.

Herman had probably suffered an accident, another one, she was barely informed, during an inspection flight in the highlands, north of Chiang Mai, and as she could guess, that jungle and rugged territory made access very difficult.

"All is not lost, Mrs. Markis". —stammered the one in civilian clothes—. "We can still find him safe, healthy and..."

"I thank you, gentlemen, for your interest in making this easier, but I prefer the truth as it is, no shenanigans".

It wasn't stoicism, Ana was not a Taoist or anything like that, it was simply the certainty that Herman had, he'd wanted, to say it properly, to end it like that, and she knew it —she always knew it after he suffered those terrible wounds in the accident, or in the war or wherever it was— and had been preparing for that in his absences.

"Well, we think he's dead but we still can't confirm it".

"We're not sure, you know", said another that until that moment hadn't said anything.

"When... when will you tell me with certainty, as you say?"

"As soon as we can, Mrs. Markis, but don't lose hope".

They all stood up. Evidently, it was over.

"We'll keep in touch, Mrs. Markis".

He thanked them and returned to her house to wait, resigned, the outcome of all that business, which seemed more and more like a useless charade.

That night, a long night, after calming and laying the children down, Suyin lit some fragrant candles, burned a bar of incense, prayed to her *phi,* and went to the kitchen to prepare Ana María a broth. As she took it, sip after sip, Ana María learned, to her surprise, that Suyin was the widow of a man she had not married.

Suyin spoke little and her past was dark, but that night, such a bitter night, Ana felt that at last she began to open up, to jump the cultural, idiomatic and social barriers that could separate them and how difficult they were to break for such an introverted and proud people.

Three days later they confirmed Herman's death and assured her that his remains would be delivered if they were recovered, which they didn't take for granted.

What hurt her most was knowing that several of her colleagues at the American School already knew the news, certainly since the day before, or even earlier.

It was the husband of Dr. Sirikit, who, although retired from active service, still had access in the Army and the Agency, at its behest —he was on fire for the way these miserable people treated his friend— told her the whole story that they wanted to hide and that Ana demanded after swearing to protect his anonymity.

The story was simple and not at all surprising to her.

Herman was actively involved in the transfer of Hmong refugees, mainly women, children and some elderly people, for several months, across the Mekong River to the west, that is, to the highlands of Thailand, where an agreement to give shelter to these unhappy ones was already made as long as the Americans made possible their later exit. But at the same time Herman was involved, even beyond his powers and the approval of his commanders, in the supplying —smuggling would be a more accurate way to say it— of rifles, ammunition and explosives to the east, towards the central Laotian mountain range where there resisted, in isolated focal points, the last Hmong warriors, if one could call warriors those hungry and malnourished – though in truth, still very dangerous– lethal beings.

What was worse, what upset those above him, was that Herman crossed the river and penetrated again and again Laos, neutral territory, or enemy territory, what the hell, carrying out missions that no one had given him.

Por la libre, as Cubans said.

The Agency had dismissed the Hmong as a people and as a fighting force, and Herman was bringing them back and armed and reconverting them into a thorn in the shoe for the Viet and the Pathet Lao, just when everyone wanted to end it all and turn the page, forget.

And what Herman was doing, in the paradoxes of war and life, also made the Hmong a thorn in the shoe for the Thai Kingdom and the Americans.

Bad news for the Western military command and for the Agency.

One stormy morning, at the height of the monsoon season, appeared in Chiang Khong, one of the head passages of the Mekong on the Thai side, the respected Hmong chief Tobey Pao, whom for the Agency people had been dead for weeks. And he didn't come alone, the guerrilla bastard brought, in a small canvas stretcher tied to a stick a little more than a meter long, what remained of the torn body of Herman Markis, dismembered by the direct impact of a 120 mortar shell from the Viet.

After healing his wounds, Tobey had bits of shrapnel embedded in the skin that covered most of his body, a bullet in the left shoulder blade and a bayonet wound on one cheek, he demanded to see a white boss to give him important information.

"Only an American boss, okay!"

Knowing him as they knew him and seeing him return from the other world in such a condition, a white boss was sought without delay.

The Agency liaison, a tall, gawky southerner who Tobey knew very well from previous interviews and strange adventures, squatted in front of him and waited, knowing that with the Hmong the excess of words was counterproductive.

"Here, sir, is the dog tag of Chief Markis". —He put it in the gringo's hand—. "What remained of him is also at your disposal, your men have him in the infirmary".

The American nodded.

Tobey waited silently for the American to keep Herman's important (important to the family) dog tag in his pocket. Then he said:

"And two 50-gauge shells". —He showed the man a bronze sheath in each hand—. In this one, which is opened, is written on a paper, by the hand of the boss Markis, the coordinates of a large armored Viet group, tanks and cannons, moving south, heading for Hanoi, I suppose.

He handed the cartridge to him without the pellets and with a sheet of onion paper rolled inside to the Agency man.

"What you do with that information, sir, I do not care, because those armored cars are not destined, for once, to crush my people".

The American nodded again without a word.

"And in this other sheath, which is crushed by its mouth, is a note from Chief Herman to his wife".

The man stared fixedly at the two metal objects, the one he already had in his hand and the one the Hmong showed him.

Tobey looked at the guy with wrinkled eyes, like two lines.

"I hope, sir, you bring it to its destination as it is". —He gave the man the crumpled metal tube with parsimony—. "It is the will of a dead man, sir, and that does matter to me, very much!" —The American leaned back, imperceptibly, at Tobey Pao's hard stare—. "The will of the man who dies in battle is sacred, sir, and you know it!"

"I know, Tobey, I know it very well... it will be done".

In the afternoon of the following day the two young ones went to pick up Ana María, went to the newly opened George Washington Memorial Parkway —traffic wasn't heavy at that time— leaving the Potomac River on the right, towards Langley, and arriving in a couple of minutes at the Agency's modern, solid gray building.

After passing the strict controls, walking long lonely corridors and going up or down, Ana was somewhat confused for such details, they entered a small hall, a kind of theater with a small stage in which were planted two flags, The United States flag on one side and the Agency flag on the other, and a few seats, perhaps twenty.

Two people were waiting for her inside. Only two.

In a secret and very brief ceremony, only a few words were said, no more than a minute or two, by the tall, blond man in a light suit, Mr. Theodore Shackley, and a three-star general of the Air Force. They then presented to Ana María, with solemnity, a medal, a gold star, in a wine-colored case.

The award, a distinguished service of the special services, with the name Herman Markis engraved on the metal, was conferred to very few, and also represented more benefits for the relatives of the condecorated deceased.

She took it in her hands, looked at it for a minute, kissed it and handed it back to the general.

She didn't shed a tear, but her face was pale, cerulean.

"Here it will remain, ma'am, under our custody. Rather, under the custody of the United States government, until the time comes for it to be delivered to you and your children".

"Thank you, I hope so, sir". —Her voice didn't shake as she feared.

Then Shackley pulled from his raincoat pocket an object wrapped in a blue cloth tied with a gold cord.

"This, madam, belongs to you and it will surprise you".

"Perhaps not, sir, if you ever intimated with Herman Markis".

"I didn't have that honor, ma'am, and believe that I'm very sorry".

A martial voice, perhaps from a projecting room next door, ordered attention.

They listened firmly and concentrated, in absolute silence, a recording of the United States anthem, they shook hands and Ana María was returned to the hotel, following the same lonely road but in reverse, by the same young people, less than two hours later.

The next day, very early, she would return to Bangkok, going first through Miami.

As night fell, and after taking a long bath and wrapping herself in her fluffy house robe, she asked for a pair of loaded Martinis from room service —courtesy of Uncle Sam—, she settled into an armchair, savored the drink and read, at last, the letter that had been denied her for so long:

Ana María:

I went to your country looking for adventures and glory, and I didn't find them, until I found you.
Now it's time to go, and I go happy, because I'm doing, for the first time, something good and noble with my life.
And I'm also happy because our children are in the best hands of the world Yours.
I hope to become a benign phi and obtain from the good God the gift of crossing the seas, to protect you from evil and to be able to look at you, and enjoy you, as I like so much, when you are alone, only when you are alone.
Ana María,
Go with your family and live.
Raise a toast for me, here and there, but live and be happy.
Live, Ana María, live, enjoy life and be happy.
Es una orden, coño.

Herman

She rose from her chair, wiped her tears with the back of her hand, took the other glass from the table, went to the window, looked at the twinkling stars in the night, towards the new moon, raised the two glasses of Martini at the same time and toasted:

"To you, Herman Markis, you crazy and wonderful bastard, to you!"

She gently clinked a glass with the other and drank, in one gulp, the rest of the Martini that was in hers.

She licked the last drops of the liquor and the salty tears that ran down her cheeks to end at the corners of her mouth.

She took a sip from the other glass and placed it, with love, on the night table, near where her head would rest that night.

"I will live, yes, I will live for my children, your children, Herman!" —She was sobbing now, compulsively, but she also felt a strange, placid relief.

"And maybe, sometime, I'll also live for myself, Herman Markis, but no one, you hear me, you motherfucker, no one will fuck up my life like you fucked mine!"

She cried and laughed at the same time.

"Wonderfully fucked, Herman!"

She took off her robe, threw it on the floor and threw herself into the huge bed completely naked and free, with the freedom of being alone and to know that whoever wants to enjoy you will not judge you at all.

"Here I am!" —She opened her arms and legs wide.

"Look and enjoy all you want, as I enjoy you in my head!"

"My love!"

17

BETHESDA, MARYLAND, 1979

Having clarified the pending matters related to Herman's death and establishing the economic benefits of her and her children, which were not very high but offered some degree of security, Ana María was convinced that it was time to return to her country, I mean, her adopted country, the United States.

Suyin, who had become by her loyalty and natural wisdom an indispensable relative, was ready to follow her, both for her and for the boys. Her niece, her daughter, really, and the rest of the motley family who depended of her in some way, would gain much more from remittances than the Thai could send them by staying and having difficulties in a lost village in deep Thailand.

The experience gained in those years in the American School, both in languages as in the handling of textbooks, teacher rudiments and archives, coupled with a small push from the Agency's boys, opened the door for Ana María to get a job as a librarian in a branch of the National Institute of Health, located in Bethesda, a nice peripheral suburb of the upper middle class of Washington. D.C., the capital of the country, although belonging territorially to the state of Maryland.

Máximo and Ana Donremí had been leading a good life in the late seventies Miami, a city where two worlds, two parallel and very dissimilar universes coexisted.

One was the world of the Anti-Castro effervescence, an exalted atmosphere, although much less violent than a decade ago, and expectant —Castro's government falls tomorrow, it collapses next month, if it falls, Americans will overthrow him, Americans don't want to do it, it won't fall, it will never fall, and thus to infinity—, already in the process of becoming, thanks to the passage of time and custom, in a less belligerent life form, much less warlike but more given to talk, talk and to radio forecasting, and also, why not, to the long-term economic accommodation, just in case *El Hombre, El Caballo* doesn't fall soon or will never fall.

Along with the rivalries of the Anti-Castro groups, there were ethnic and racial confrontations, as well as the first outbursts of what would be the crazy years of drug trafficking, delirious Miami Vice and the exaggerated Al Pacino's Scarface years and his exuberant and schematic Tony Montana, a Hollywood caricature (caricature, yes, but with lots of real pieces) that had its followers and imitators, its winners and losers, and of course its casualties.

But there was another world, another universe, the world of legal and hard work for the thousands and thousands of people that had to find their livelihood in Hialeah's clothing, shoes and purse factories, soft drink bottlers, spinning mills and grocery stores, in the immense '*moles*' (it comes from mall but in Cuban) that began to sprout everywhere, in the Westchester laundries, in the community services of Little Havana, building expensive and not so expensive houses, fixing ceilings, Kendall schools and Day Cares scattered throughout town, working in car shops, as police officers, firefighters, paramedics, funeral home workers, embalmers, furniture makers, preparing and serving drinks (is there a better bartender than a Cuban?) in the restaurants and bars of Coconut Grove and the Beach, a.k.a Miami Beach. And whatever it was that brought food to their table and money to pay rent, furniture in installments, the indispensable "transportation", a rattletrap whose only requirement is to go, electricity, water, telephone and a 14-carat gold with *La Virgen de la Caridad Del Cobre* or *San Lazaro*, the saint with the wooden walking stick, the sores and the dogs, hanging around the neck for good luck and a little for ostentation, the '*figurao*'.

In that last world of stubborn and sometimes exhausting work, often more than one occupation per day and overtime on weekends, but very useful if the body was enduring and stubborn enough, was Máximo, with his physical and mental health very much recovered, among other things thanks to the care of a Nicaraguan woman, the first real female he had truly known and loved in his life.

He had had, before he went to jail, little girlfriends to squeeze in the cinemas and in their homes when the chaperons weren't looking, and perhaps two or three prostitutes, always hurried and indifferent, in their fleeting raids through the zones of tolerance of a Havana that was long gone, but that counted little as a true experience in the love life of a man.

The Nica, a shorty with strong arms and legs like logs, solid, a couple of years older than him, divorced and with two children, but committed, accustomed to see adversity to its face, and overcome it, affectionate (Nicaragua is a country of poets, don't forget) and learned in the arts of revealing to a *macho*, her *macho*, unknown continents, and to obtain them!

Ana Donremí was also in this world, who for the first time in her life worked in the street and earned a very modest but useful salary in a Cuban drugstore on *Calle 8*, where in addition of entertaining herself, making friends and helping people —she learned that many people carried their crosses and lived their own calvaries, the same or worse than hers— began to alleviate, not to forget, the pain locked in the nameless tomb of the cemetery of Havana.

She had even become talkative, but there was one exception, no politics.

"I hate them too much to talk about them, the day they fuck themselves you tell me and we'll see what I'll do, but in the meantime... don't even mention them to me!"

"And Gretel?" Well, Gretel, the young woman with the sullen gaze and the heart of gold, as always, had a special place in the heart and in the thoughts of Ana María.

Since she settled in Washington almost five years ago, Ana was trying to convince Gretel to go and live with the children, Suyin and her. There was no shortage of pretexts and pleadings to help her and Suyin with the children, to obtain a higher level of work and with a better salary, to improve her English, to leave the provincialism of Miami, to see the world and a lot of other arguments, but reality was that Ana wanted Gretel to be close to her because she needed her and because she felt the urgency of repairing an old and excessive debt, a debt that had become as evident as an explosion when she was reunited with her sister.

In fact Ana felt doubly indebted to her sister, first for having left her, in an act of compulsive madness, alone, at the head, being almost a child, of a wasted house in a completely hostile environment, averse, destroying her possibilities to overcome it and enjoy life, turning her into a devoted mother of her own mother, a widowed woman with a damaged brain and her imprisoned brother.

That was already a huge debt, but there was another.

In one of those long evenings of gossiping —just before her return to Bangkok from Miami and the death of Herman— that left them yawning and with drooping eyes all day, Gretel had decided, and it wasn't easy at all for her, to tell her sister the reason of her unhappiness, that misfortune that she chewed on without ever passing it on to others.

"Ana..." —She made a painful stop—. "Since I was a child I've liked women". —Her hands were as cold as ice—. "Can you imagine what would have happened if my father or mother had noticed that?"

Ana nodded and held her tightly in her arms.

"That was a different time, Gretel". —She kissed her on the forehead—. "But why does that matter now?"

"My father has not been present for a long time to spit in my face but my mother and brother are still there". —Her face was so pale it looked like a plaster statue—. "And the rest of society is still there, Ana, do you realize that?"

"I shit on people and society, Gretel, and I proved it, unfortunately for you, my mother and Máximo, many years ago, when I left with Herman!"

"You left with a man, but I..."

"Come with me to Washington and let them all go to hell, fuck them!" —She stroked her head with a hand that shook from anger—. "Love them very much from afar, Gretel, from very far away!"

"What I suffered there, Ana, in that society of male abusers with an inferiority complex and submissive women and what I can suffer here, where the same people are, with the same complexes or worse, with the same hypocrisy, is not what matters to me, Ana". —Two tears ran down her face—. "It's..."

"What is it, Gretel?" —She gripped her arms tightly—. "They can't sway me!"

"There's nothing you can do".

Gretel burst open like a cataract, and suddenly Ana realized, with such force that she felt it as a kick to the stomach, the horror Gretel had suffered, not having for years and years someone to be honest with, whom to cry, no one to ask for help, not to have been able to hit walls and break the crockery, to live pretending all the time in an environment where everything, absolutely everything, even fucking politics, were adverse to her.

She told Ana of her shortcomings, her terrors, told her that she had had some romance, more platonic than real, some little adventure, a touch of hands, a smile, a rejection today, a kiss flown tomorrow, an ambiguous word that left her breathless and she had been living like that until she met a girl, a young puppet maker —a stage girl, as the assholes who swam in that village of idiots and simulators told her— that brought her daughter —a girl born of a relationship she had out of boredom with another boy like her while they were picking grapefruit in a school in the countryside where chaos ruled and sex was free— for her to teach math.

"It was a love like yours for Herman, Ana, it was crazy!"

For the first time in her life she had been happy, really happy, and then, just then, they released Máximo from prison and they had to get her stuff out in one day.

"I couldn't say goodbye to her, she came running, desperate, like a madwoman to see me, to cry with me and found that there were four or five policemen and a couple of neighbors out front, and our mother too, Ana". —Her whole body trembled—. I gave her a notebook with poems by Neruda, Kavafis, Lorca and I don't know who else —everything of any material value that could have been in the house that was now owned by the state— and I begged her to run away so she wouldn't be marked.

"Can you understand the sense of loss, the emptiness I feel inside, Ana? "—She blew her nose to calm herself—. "Yes, of course you do, you too have lost your husband!"

"No Gretel, Herman and I really loved each other, that gets to me, but it wasn't the same anymore". Her eyes clouded. "You have no idea how smart that American was, when everything began to become a routine, when custom and tedium began to kill us he had the balls to fix things up to make us all comfortable, and left without saying goodbye, or he did, someday I'll give you something for you to read, and you'll know, I'll tell you what that madman was capable of doing".

"To us, Ana, to my stage girl and I life didn't leave any room for routine".

"Have you heard something about her?"

"Yes, sometimes we talk on the phone". —Gretel was the living picture of despair—. "At first it was very difficult but now calls are made through a third country and people are beginning to go there". —She shook her head—. "They say they are going to allow week-long trips and stuff like that".

"She can't come?"

"That's very difficult, impossible for now, and she has a daughter who is almost a teenager". —She rubbed her eyes—. "The father would have to give permission for the girl to travel and I don't know if he would be willing to do so".

"Shit!"

"Do you understand why I don't want to leave Miami?"

"Can you do something, with money, with someone you know, with whoever, anything?"

"It isn't a matter of money or friends, it's a matter of time, Ana, life goes on, years go by".

In the living room of her cozy apartment on a side street of Bradley Boulevard, very close to Bethesda Row, the modern and cozy square where they walked to buy ice cream and fresh bread on weekends, Ana María hung up the phone after talking with her sister for a while, just like they did almost every night.

Gretel was doing well, she worked hard, studied, earned her money.

"How the fuck will she do all right if she's getting old and her heart is broken!"

The punch in the wall ran like a wave through the rest of the house.

Suyin jumped on the couch where she used to sit, straight and very quiet, watching music shows on the TV.

Ana María ignored her, got up, went to the kitchen and prepared a Martini, a dry and well loaded Martini, and walked to the balcony.

She looked at the moon, shining through the passing clouds.

"Herman, you crazy American, madman of my soul, if you're a *phi* with powers, and I know you are, dammit Herman, do something for my sister!"

She drunk the Martini almost without breathing, except for a little that remained in the bottom of the glass.

"Cross the sea and do it, Herman, for me, I beg you!"

She tossed the little bit of the Martini over the flower bed that adorned one side of the balcony.

"Do it, please, do it for her, and for me!"

"You fucking American, do it, please!"

"Fucking do it!"

18

LA HABANA, 1980

The news, which exploded like a cluster bomb, began to spread throughout Havana, all over Cuba, around Miami, around the world, at a time when there was apparently no information loophole on the island, State control was impenetrable, or so it was said, all the press, radio and television were of the State, there was only one phone company, of the State, of course, and Internet was about to be invented and social networks weren't even dreamt of.

If they had existed in that time, can you imagine?

But the power of word of mouth, *radiobemba* as Cubans said, immediately challenged and surpassed coercive measures, prohibitions, denunciations and even the laws of physics.

The event sounded very strange, really unusual, but yes, it was happening —an unexpected event was occurring, and great, like a television commercial of some product would say, in four words, what was in the minds of the people: "Something big is going on!".

A group of ordinary, unarmed Cubans had stolen a public service bus, a guagua —the driver of which was one of them— in a neighborhood that was relatively isolated from the periphery of Havana, and had forcibly entered, demolishing the fence with the vehicle, in the building that occupied an Embassy of a Latin American country, Peru, and requested, he and all the passengers, political asylum.

In one unclear incident, one of the surveillance police men, belonging to Cuban security, had been shot dead at the event. The government claimed that he had been murdered by the asylees but the voice of the street echoed that he had been hit by the cross-fire of his own companions in the diplomatic surveillance unit.

The Castro government had asked the Ambassador to hand over the refugees immediately, including some women and teenagers, and he had refused, in an unprecedented attitude of a Latin American diplomat (supposedly all of them, including their governments, feared Castro), claiming that being returned to the police ran the risk, the certainty, rather, of being executed without the right to a fair trial.

Castro, in a fit of anger, had ordered the guards who guarded the legation to be removed and to allow people to enter freely. The measure, unprecedented in Cuban politics, was provoking an avalanche of people of all sexes and ages, oh, and from all parts of the national territory, into the diplomatic building.

"This idiot will learn to respect me!", It is said that Castro said this in a fit of uncontrollable rage.

And the 'idiot' learned what it means to have thousands and thousands of people standing, crammed against each other, unable to move, sweating, pissing and shitting the place, with no water or food, some dared even to have sex, in the space, the brief space, of a two-story house for a normal family, two garages, two or three offices, a garden and some employees.

For a couple of years some exiles had been going, from Miami and some other cities to Havana. Many requirements were demanded and not all those requesting it were accepted, but that limited openness had made evident the economic contrast between one group and the other, favoring, of course, those on the American side. Exacerbating the desire of thousands of Cubans in the island to emigrate, to leave, to not get used to it as the popular joke said, but leave, get out, to fly, to flee, to set foot on the neighbor in the North.

And here it was, in the sight of the world, now, the result.

Ana María, who more or less followed the international news, but heard the unexpected incident in her work, phoned Gretel.

"What's happening in Cuba, Gretel? What have you heard?"

"Nobody knows exactly, Ana María, but it seems that something serious, exceptional, is happening".

"Have you talked with your friend?"

"Not with her, the telephone lines are crowded, but I've been able to talk to some people and everyone think that this can make the government open its hand, I mean the exits, or who knows, perhaps to shut the doors closed even more".

"Don't be so pessimistic, *chica*."

"It's been so long, Ana, of stumbling upon the same stones".

"What are you going to do, mi *hermana*?"

"Last year I tried to go and was denied entry, as you know, perhaps because of being my father's daughter and my brother's sister". —Her voice faltered a little, but she quickly recovered—. "They never explained the reason, but I'm trying again". —She drew a deep breath—. "My fingers are crossed and I touch my navel every few minutes".

Ana smiled:

"Keep me posted, mi *hermanita*, that I live in another world, but you know that I'm here to help you, Gretel, in anyway".

"I know, Ana".

"Whatever you need, Gretel, anything, you just say it".

In less than three days more than ten thousand people had entered the Embassy, occupying even the roofs (some were injured or killed when falling), the few bathrooms, bedrooms, living rooms, kitchen, pantry, the cistern, the library, a small wine cellar —which of course they drank— leaving not a single millimeter free and putting the government in a mess, with its own people, with its people, with the international press, with the friendly governments, the Americans, the Russians, a mess that to get out of was going to require a lot of skill, all the mythological ability and luck of Fidel Castro.

And Castro, of course, was a cheating, manipulative, extraordinarily daring guy.

And sneaky.

The cynical, Machiavellian analysis (a strategic politician he would say to his closest associates) was simple:

First, the Cuban exiles in Miami would do anything to get their families out of Cuba, and they could move money and resources that they would look for even under the stones, there was no doubt about it.

Second, people would leave happily, leaving everything, houses, cars, clothes, electrical equipment, dishes, children's toys, behind, thus freeing the government from labor pressure, housing shortages, Public transport and food. With time you would have to put a limit, of course, but one would see how to do that on the fly.

Third, the political cost of his government would be high, but this could be remedied by the announcement that the disaffected fugitives were the worst of the old society (the twenty-one years since that 'old society' disappeared would soon be forgotten) and Carter, the peanut seller Jimmy Carter, the American President, was a poor fool who prayed to his God all the time and prayed about that human rights idiocy, and as they say in Cuba: *un perfecto comemierda*.

The secret was in that it had to be the Cubans in Miami the ones who pressured the Americans.

Cuba would let them go, but would the gringos accept them?

"Do you accept them?" "Yes".

"Go ahead then".

A port would be set up so that the people in Miami would come to get, by their own means, of course, those who would like to leave. Oh, and this would not be made public, but it would be used to send the Americans a few thousand prisoners, common criminals, murderers, pedophiles, rapists, thieves, pickpockets and another bunch of crazy, the most fucked up in the head, the most dangerous, removed from insane asylums.

The Americans were going to learn how bad the slags that capitalism and the bourgeoisie had created before the Revolution, it didn't matter, of course, that many of them weren't even born on that time.

But this was not a subject to discuss.

"Let the gringos have them!", said Castro.

"Let the scum go!"

"Let them go!"

There was only one problem, a small inconvenience, that the Embassy building couldn't even fit a needle and the stream of people kept coming.

"Well, those who want to go have to be registered in their neighborhoods".

"Just like that, Commander?"

"No, they'll pay the price of repudiation from honest citizens".

"All right, first repudiation, and then we let them go".

First the eggs against the doors and walls, the offensive yells, the blows, the spit, the infernal noise so that they can't rest or sleep, to destroy the furniture and the bed clothes, to strip them in the street, to offend them, to humiliate them, fouling them with shit, peeing them, marking houses with paint, raping them.

"Not that last one, that's a crime".

"That's right, sorry, Commander, why not feather them?"

'No, not that, that was what the Ku Klux Klan did to blacks, and we are not like those motherfucking gringos".

"True, and kill them?"

"No chico, are you dumb or what? Let them become a heavy burden for the Americans, for the politicians there, let them leave".

"Let's, then!"

"Yes, let them go, let the scum go".

"Let them go".

19

PORT OF MARIEL, 1980

A na María heard from Gretel again when she was staying in a little motel in Key West —*Cayo Hueso*, as the Cubans baptized that islet located at the southernmost tip of Florida, during the wars of independence against Spain—, first she was acknowledging the terrain, crowded with nervous and desperate people, a disturbed place, disturbed by the shouting of sailors who offered their boats. Then negotiating with a Cuban-American boatman, apparently well known in that world, which everyone there called Papito.

Papito was one of those Cubans that had fled the island, fled Castro, rather, and came to the United States very young, teenagers made men in the early sixties and lacking economic resources. With one hand in front and the other behind, they learned English on the street, and most important, they developed their inventiveness and their innate ability to make money by any means necessary, literally. Although Papito had a bonus, he had enrolled in the Army and had made a tour, from 68 to 70, in one of the harshest and most bloody stages of the Vietnam War. In that fight, he had won a purple heart for a bullet wound on a buttock —he wasn't running, he told his friends— and an honorable discharge with very favorable mentions in his file.

The ship of Papito, an old Bertram yacht of about forty feet in length, had been acquired between three partners, two Cubans and one Colombian, thinking about the great business that was coming, what was more, it was already making rich the most lucid and risky: marijuana traffic from Colombia or the somewhat closer Panama. But now, all of a sudden, this was about bringing people in from the Port of Mariel on the north coast of Cuba to Key West, and the migrants' relatives paid in cash. Oh, and showing patriotism, very quickly, while it lasted, because with Castro one could not count on the future beyond 24 hours.

Papito was a nice guy, energetic, attractive, a jokester, open. He wasn't a fresh guy or daring with women, not at all, and although he knew that he was likable, Papito considered himself a perfect gentleman. But that Ms., or Mrs., she was well in her years, negotiated her affairs alone, with no husband or man to accompany her, and although a little sullen, quite original. A single and original woman, according to the Jamaican, absolute fan and a good guitar player of Reggae, that supplied the boat of provisions and fuel to Papito.

Tall, strong, black-haired, snub-nosed, a big and well formed mouth, straight back and hands and big tits and hard, brother, hard as marble! And what buttocks, sir, to rub them and to give them a good spanking! An athlete or a butch, what the hell.

But let's get to business.

The deal was simple.

The relatives in the United States paid $5,000 dollars for each person that they brought in the boat, twenty five hundred before and the other half after. If the relative didn't come —it was known that the Cuban government didn't let everyone go— the money was lost.

The migratory arrangements had to be taken cared of by the possible passengers in Cuba and their relatives in Miami and the boatman, Papito in this case, but there were hundreds lurking around, he simply transported them across the strait. If someone from Miami wanted to go on the boat, both on the way in and on the way back, he or she had to pay for his or her five thousand «dolores», because he or she took up space.

And Gretel had to go on the boat because her efforts to obtain a Cuban passport and an entry visa —to her own country, dammit!— were still being delayed.

Máximo, who wasn't at all interested in what was going on in Cuba —he heard the news and comments on the radio, and sometimes expressed opinions among some acquaintances and clients, but nothing more— was making good money in the laundry that he opened in Hialeah together with his Nicaraguan woman (the idea had been hers) with whom he had two children, and with hers there were four, and worked, my God how they worked! He worked without rest, which allowed him to help everybody in the two families, his and especially his wife's, who were living in the new Sandinista Nicaragua.

Máximo was a conservative type, austere, reminiscences of jail, he said, but always giving a helping hand to the one that needed it.

"Gretel, here's a thousand dollars, it's not a loan, it's a gift". —He hugged his sister affectionately—. "I don't care what you're going to do in that place, but be very careful". —Deferential and careful, he didn't mention the late Rubino and himself and his nefarious experiences—. "And be careful also of what you bring here".

The Nicaraguan, a family acquisition, interrupted:

"Your sister knows what she's doing, Máximo, don't impose conditions on her".

"No, I'm not imposing any conditions, God forgive me if I do, I love her too much and I owe her too much to do that, but I'm advising her with all my heart". —He squeezed her into his arms again—. "She's too noble, my little sister, too selfless".

Ana Donremí didn't ask, she preferred not to know, nor did she resist.

"See if you can bring the remains of your father".

She feinted an affectionate gesture.

"If they'd let me go there to get them out of that hole and bring them here, I'd even go to that goddamn place". —She put a little envelope in a pocket of Gretel's baggy blouse—. "I'm not rich, you know this, but here you have something for the trip".

Ana María sent her five thousand dollars and the rest Gretel took out of her savings.

Gretel's pretext for that crazy voyage? She didn't think of any, let everyone think what they wanted. She only lied to her mother and brother the real amount of money she needed, and asked Ana María, which wasn't necessary, not to tell anyone what she had given her.

"It's like a war trip to do journalism, mi *hermana*, just to see how things are and nothing else".

"God be with you, Gretel, you know what you're doing!"

Ana María wasn't so sure that Gretel knew what she was doing, doubt was eating her, but she would never interfere, never, after having abandoned her for years and years, which weighed in her soul like a cannonball.

Papito and her, no more crew, threw themselves into the adventure. He boasted of his skills as a sailsman and it seemed that he wasn't misguided.

"If I dodged, and very well, the bullets of the Viet Cong as an army boatman in the Mekong Delta, how the fuck am I not going to sail this shitty little boat myself?"

They left in a dark dawn and with a fairly thick sea, without being choppy, but very rocky for those who weren't used to it.

In spite of the waves, the sharp wind and the flow towards the east, in the opposite direction, from the Gulf Stream, the old friend and companion of the eccentric and drunkard Hemingway, the crossing of the strait was advancing very well.

At dawn, far from the coast of departure and much closer to the arrival, Papito gave Gretel, dizzy and kind of dopey from the heavy sleep of a sleepless night, a cup of loaded black coffee and a soft and wet kiss at the nape of her neck, lifting her hair with his warm and calloused man's hand made by the vicissitudes of life.

Gretel jumped, took a sip of the coffee, burned her tongue, woke up completely, put the cup on the compass base, stood up like a bolt of lightning, grabbed a red ax with both hands that was kept in a cabinet in the main cabin and planted herself in front of a Papito, caught out of balance, perplexed.

"If you touch me again I'll break your skull in two and throw you in the water!"

"Damn, you're not well in the head, *niña*!"

"I'm better than you think, comemierda!"

"I gave you a kiss of affection to wake you up, *coño*, not from man to woman!"

"And I'll give you an ax blow from man to man if you touch me again, you asshole!"

That encounter, taking an unexpected turn, forever sealed the friendship of Papito and Gretel, two warriors of different wars. There would be no sex, Papito was no fool and knew his limits. Gretel, accustomed to cheap machismo and mockery, could recognize the man who showed strength, but didn't enforce it.

"Bury the ax, *niña*, like the American Indians, I just wanted to give you some friendly warmth to relieve your loneliness!"

"I'll keep it, but close to me". —She smiled at him—. "I like you as a friend, Papito, but don't go beyond that even by a millimeter. Is that clear?"

"Dea"l.

"Deal".

They shook hands.

"Help me get my friend out of that hell".

"I'll help you, but help me to put in line the herd of wild animals that are going to be forced on us to bring in the boat". —He pointed to the stern—. "Those bastards" —he pointed with his index finger the still invisible but already near coast of the island—, they're putting in the boats much more people that can fit and they say that some of these people are crazies and outlaws.

"I heard them say that on the Key". —She slowly brought the ax back to its place—. "Of course I'll help you, Papito, count on me, I'm your crew member, right?"

"After seeing you with that iron in your hands, I don't doubt it, *mi niña*, I don't doubt it as my name is Papito!"

They were anchored for eleven days, hovering in the center of the bay of Mariel, surrounded by hundreds of motor boats, yachts, shrimp boats, tugboats, barges, and all that could cross the strait in both directions. Some ships, about ten, capsized on the voyage back, and even today the number of those who perished by drowning and were never found is unknown, but that belongs to history.

Gretel wasn't allowed to go ashore, although Cuban immigration officials met with her on the boat —they went from boat to boat in a Cuban Navy motorboat— and collected all the necessary data from the two people for which she came for. They clarified that the aforementioned persons have to agree to leave the country and that if there were any minors involved, both parents have to authorize the departure.

On the tenth day of waiting, they brought the woman and her daughter. There were more than fifty people on the yacht when they arrived, but the woman and her daughter came with a companion, the girl's father, a common and ordinary guy, simple, the typical uproot of the system, vulgar and uneducated.

It was like a bucket of ice water for Gretel, not because of the man's presence, which was predictable for them to get permission for the minor, definitely a teenager now, but by a sudden and surprising disappointment, something that she couldn't explain.

She saw her as being shallow, dull, even dumb, taking care of form with her husband and with her, with both at the same time, alleging in a low voice that with the girl in front she couldn't express herself and that it wasn't convenient that that, the brief relationship they had once, was made public among so many people. Or she changed a lot, or she, Gretel, had idealized her from the distance. Or did time, that murderer, have passed over them like a steel rolling pin?

Gretel placed them, the woman, the girl and the husband —the guy was very expressively happy to have arrived there, even if he swallowed his tongue when Cuban immigration showed— in a dry and somewhat more protected place, she said a few words of encouragement to her, after a soulless stroke of hands, and she was set to help Papito with dedication to keep order and control that chaos as if she were a crew member with the experience of a whole marine life.

The return journey was difficult.

Papito, once away from the Cuban military boats, pulled an AR-15 rifle out of some hidden place, told Gretel that the ax was a useless device among so many people and he placed in her hand a shiny, new, impressive black Glock handgun.

"With this you can kill me more cleanly than with the ax, Gretel, but I don't advise it, at least as long as the return from hell lasts".

With those irons of fear in their hands and with the help of two or three refugees who offered to lend a helping hand —for years they kept in contact with a young man in Miami, a decent and organized guy, a student of something related with medicine, now a wealthy trader, who told them he was nicknamed Yiyo, perhaps a forerunner of the subsequent epidemic of names with 'Y' like Yoani, Yoandri, Yuriorkis, Yurisleydis, Yusnavy, Yuselen and dozens more that ravaged the Cubans in the years to come—, they maintained order among the 134 people that crowded in the cabins and the hold, among them several schizophrenics without treatment —a Cuban guard warned them in a low voice— and three or four declared murderers who their handcuffs were taken off as soon as they pushed them towards the boat.

Both Papito and Gretel had to shoot to the air several times to prevent those individuals from raping women or killing each other in quarrels —they even tried to drink the boat's fuel in the absence of something better to do than to just lie down— but blood, luckily, wasn't shed and it wasn't necessary to throw no one to the sea. Although Papito was about to do it with an all tattooed guy, jail meat, that was very close to becoming uncontrollable and that showed his penis to Gretel and the other women on board.

Papito pointed the AR-15 to the man's balls, a madman or a junkie, he pointed and fired, making a lateral movement, a short blast over the edge and with an icy aplomb (apparent, according to Gretel, very real, according to him) said in a low but resonant voice for the silence that was made in the boat:

"I'll start with the dick, so that it hurts, and finish with the head, and then we throw you to the sharks, so that they feed with your carrion, you fucker, if they have their guts really hard so they can digest your skin!"

The man, as if the nurses of the asylum had sedated him, spent the rest of the journey in a corner and took great care of peeing so that there would be no misunderstandings with the madman with the machine gun (he was the crazy one!) and the little bitch with the handgun.

Papito, additionally, lost Gretel's five thousand dollars, because he refused to collect them.

"You should charge me for your work as sailor, crewwoman, helmswoman, radio-telegrapher, co-pilot, alarm clock, cook, policewoman, shit cleaner, shrink and everything else".

"You're an idiot, Papito".

"I'm your friend, *niña*, don't be stupid".

"Don't insult me or I'll shoot you in the belly and throw you into the water".

"I haven't shown you my parts for you to do that to me".

"Ha, I knew it! You're embarrassed by the size of that guy's thing!"

"Ah, yes, do it then, shoot me in the belly and thus you'll learn by your own and the hard way to take this floating shell to port and to dominate that stupid army".

"Okay, you win, but behave yourself".

Papito, insightful, knew from the beginning what had happened, but he had the subtlety of not making even one comment.

And so, with shrieks, screams, scares, dizziness, the runs, vomiting, insults, shots to the air, punches, thunders, downpours, hunger, thirst, anxiety, they arrived at the port.

"I didn't think we were going to get here alive", Papito said, puffing with relief.

"I brought you back, Papito, I brought you back!"

He smiled at her with his white teeth:

"Yes, *mi niña*, that's true, you alone brought me back".

"Are you recognizing it?"

"Yes, I admit it, I came back walking, wandering in the scenes, and even shopping in the luxury stores of Havana".

She kissed him, like a sister, on the cheek.

In the middle of the afternoon, with the sun coming down, they docked.

Exhausted, but relieved, one could even say happy.

20

KEY WEST, 1980

Anchored at a crowded jetty at the Key West dock, and having finished the sweeping process through which the American Immigration Service took over 134 refugees who were wondering how they alone had been able to bring them from Cuba. In the group were, of course, Gretel's friend, the daughter who was a thin mulatto, and the husband, an ordinary fellow, a lout who had expressed his content by not giving a fuck about those who had stayed behind on the island, a celebration that lasted until two American soldiers — there were dozens there to enforce order— shut him up with a very bad face and unequivocal gestures of displeasure that included a kick in the ass with the metal toe of a Marine boot, which throwed the guy onto the dockboard.

Papito and Gretel suddenly realized, there wasn't time for that before, the overwhelming dirt and the damage that had to be cleaned and repaired on the ship and even themselves.

The atrocious exhaustion of days and days without rest, without sleep, taking naps of ten minutes and separately, so that one of the two stood with eyes wide open, without a moment of calm, aware of the time, Caribbean summer squalls, tides, the level of fuel in the tanks, the darkness, and the worst, Cuban officials who were struggling to push more and more people into the crowded boat and then the bunch of savages that terrorized the rest, the great majority of the passengers, and themselves, in spite of the AR-15, the Glock and the balls both had, although they faltered sometimes they had to confront them to maintain the order and avoid ending at the bottom of the Florida Strait or in a jail on either side of the canal.

"We made it, Gretel, wiped out, but we made it!"

"We aren't dreaming, right, Papito?"

The friend, now a well-known acquaintance of Gretel, pulling her stupid and now frightened husband by the arm, had shouted at her that she would call her, if she could, for she had no idea where they were being taken, as soon as she could, to see each other and talk.

"We need your help, Gretel, don't abandon us". —She grasped the girl's other hand so she wouldn't get lost in the crowd—. "I'll explain everything when I have the time".

"Don't worry, *mijita*, I'll wait for your call".

Papito had never seen Gretel, in the three weeks they had spent together, put on a face so blank, so empty, so distant from everything, like someone who had reached the Tao (he learned about that in the Mekong Delta from a dying South Vietnamese sergeant and from a card-shooter in Saigon) but wisely swallowed his tongue and made no comment, none, alluding to the rough subject.

They tied the ropes to fix the boat to the dock, put their weapons in their hiding places, and made sure they were out of reach of any stranger, cut off the energy from the accumulators, closed the hatches that could be closed and weren't unhinged, unclogged the bilge, tightened the wheel of the rudder, turned off the radar and looked like two runners who would have finished, and won, a full marathon.

He helped her leap to the jetty and followed her with agility.

"I've been out there for twenty days without putting my feet on dry land, Papito, everything's spinning!"

"I'm the same, Gretel".

"I'm so tired, *coño*, I'm realizing it now!"

"And I'm beat, Gretel, and we need to clean the tons of shit that's inside the boat with a hose, take away the vomit and foul smell, check the damage, re-tune the engines and then take it to Miami, and then finish collecting what we..."

"Shut up already, Papito, I'm fainting by just hearing you". —She stumbled between the boards, and he held her with both hands—. "I owe you money too".

"Now you work on my boat and for me so we're even, *mi niña*". —He helped her up to a few wooden steps, four or five, which led to an open-air café-bar—. "Let's have a cold beer, *niña*, my treat".

"The thirst, the hunger, left me long ago, Papito, I have the stomach destroyed by eating canned food, drinking brackish water and crap!"

He helped her gently sit on the last rung, brought two beers from the bar, and sat down next to her, very close, but without exaggerating.

They clinked their bottles reluctantly.

"We're tired as hell, but we're rich, Gretel, you know?"

"You're the millionaire, not me, and besides I owe you money".

"Cut that shit out, Gretel". —He took a long drink—. "You're courageous, I didn't think you could deal with those beasts like you did". —He leaned forward a little—. "My best adventure has been to have met you, and I'm not lying to you, I've had very good adventures around the world".

"Don't exaggerate, Papito, you're telling me that because deep down you still have the desire to sleep with me".

"I have a lot of imagination, and hands, *niña*".

"You are depraved, Papito, a degenerate".

"It's possible, and you're cute".

She put the bottle on the plank floor, rested over his thighs, curled up between his legs and burst into tears, with sobs, with little wails, as she hadn't done for a long time.

He put his fingers in her black hair.

"What's the matter, *mi niña*".

"You know what, Papito, you're not stupid". —She slowly calmed down—. "I did all this for nothing!"

He kissed her on the back of her neck with a soft, rich tenderness.

"I asked my family for money, I made fun of their advice, I cheated them, I deceived myself, I was mentally retarded, like I've always been!"

"It'll pass, *mi niña*, in the delta, lying in a mangrove, there was a night when I was sure that it wasn't dawning, until the Viet Cong passed me over and they stepped on me with their rubber sandals". —He ran a dirty hand over his forehead—. "One of those shitty chinamen stood on top of me and took a piss on my back, and look, here I am".

"You and that fucking delta, Papito!"

"Let me win one at least, *niña*!"

"And don't call me a fucking *niña* anymore, I'm thirty-four years old!"

"To me you're a *niña*!"

She thrust her face deeper between his legs, perhaps to dry her tears, or to hide from the world, to hide from the sight of human beings, to flee.

"I don't know, Papito, my head is spinning". —She sniffled—. "Now I just want to sleep, forget everything, let go". —She put her other arm around his thighs.

"You're tired, beat, that's all".

He kissed her on the back of the neck again.

"I want to sleep Papito... forget everything and sleep... but with you".

He caressed her hair that had grown in the three weeks of battle. Soft, very soft, with infinite patience; then helped her up, held her, walked slowly, close together, two or three blocks, until they found a small, pretty-looking motel (there'd be a time to come for the modern four and five stars that exist today on the Key) they entered and he paid in cash —this were times when no one asked questions— for a room (the best one you have, brother!) to the gringuito with the folder and they left, the two of them, very close, step by step, up the stairs.

The room was small but tolerable, and above all it had a good shower and very hot water.

He undressed her with exquisite care, took off her sneakers and thick socks with a dry sweat smell, the dirty t-shirt that had been white aeons ago, the jeans, the pink bra that she didn't need, her pants, he smelled it with mischief and it smelled of herbs or something like that, put her in the bathtub, almost lifted her up, let the hot water run all over her body, and what a body, and lathered her like a little girl, head, armpits, back, buttocks, everything, washed her for a while with warm water, wrapped her in a huge beach towel, rubbed her a bit to dry and warm her and carried her, slowly, towards the bed.

He was dirty, soaked and happy.

He rapidly undressed and threw all the clothes to the corner, next to hers.

"Come back Papito". —She was face down, limp and almost asleep. Papito stepped into the shower and lathered himself until he shined. He couldn't believe how much dirt he had on him or what was waiting for him in bed.

He dried himself fast, with energy, but without showing hurry or anxiety.

It was dark now.

He looked at her for a minute, half-wrapped in the towel and breathing quietly. My God, she was thirty-four years old and looked like twenty!

He got into the bed, slowly, holding his breath, not turning the light on.

"Come". —She drew him with one arm towards her.

He kissed her on the back, the shoulders, turned her slowly, kissed her carefully on her breasts, brushing them with his lips as if they were rose petals.

"Do it slowly, Papito, I'm not used to this". —She whispered in his ear.

There was music on the street, New York salsa, disco music, Bee Gees, Abba, laughter and voices, people, Boney M, joyful drunks and tourists who saw, commented and photographed, that invasion of disgruntled Cubans, emaciated, frozen with dampness and cold, hungry, dizzy, frightened like rabbits of the unknown, the unexplored, on a longed for country, yearned for years but at the same time strange and dreadful.

An adventure for the usual visitors of the Keys and the passing tourists that had suddenly become unique, unpublished, incredible and truly historical.

"You'd better sleep, kid". —He tried to cover her ears with his hands.

"No, hug me". —She stuck to him with a strange force, with an unknown eagerness.

He kissed her face and she kissed him back on the mouth, tongue and all.

She was wise, the bitch! Thought Papito.

"Slowly, Papito, soft, I'm not a virgin, but I'm a lady".

"As you wish, *mi niña*".

He penetrated her carefully, with fear, little by little, in slow motion. She was tight, but moist, he couldn't remember having been with a young lady and didn't recognize the difference, but she was delicious.

He kissed her neck.

"You're good, Papito". —She sighed.

He thought of the dead of the Delta, the sound of bullets hitting the armor of the boat, the movies of Dean Martin, the latest car models, in...

"Not yet, fuck, no...!"

He couldn't hold it anymore, less than a minute, shit! And filled her with the anxiety of three weeks, a contained anxiety, which exploded without measure.

She squeezed him, squeezed him tightly, sighed, kissed him on the ear, and fell asleep.

"There'll be another time, let's be optimistic", he thought, and pulled out slowly, settling her down.

He wrapped his body around her, began to caress her side...

And he also fell asleep.

In a few hours, it would dawn.

21

MIAMI, 1981

In the following months: July, August and September of 1980, Gretel and Papito repeated the adventure twice more, now with more experience, much more security in their abilities and better equipment, besides certain changes to the boat, like putting a thick net that allowed them to isolate themselves in the area of the helm and some extra drainages near the beams to be able to hose the shit and people if necessary.

Oh, and a shotgun, a shotgun of fear, like a life insurance for extreme cases, God forbid!

In the first trip, they brought 110 Cubans and in the second only 85.

It was evident that this couldn't continue. The international scandal was huge in the face of the onslaught of common criminals and psychiatric patients lacking all medical treatment and control that blended with the large mass of working Cubans —the millionaires and bourgeois had long since disappeared from the island scene and it was too difficult to invoke them now—, ordinary people who were still struggling to come to the United States. And the Carter administration was already beginning to give important signs of disgust, and worse, a serious disapproval in public opinion polls. Those in the know said that Politicians such as Arkansas Gov. Bill Clinton and Carter himself lost their election because of all this.

And in fact, a month later, at the end of October, the Cuban government abruptly cut off the exits and closed the port of Mariel to the motley fleet of floating shells, as Papito called them, which served as shuttles between Key West and the north coast of Pinar del Río, where the port of Mariel was located.

Papito and Gretel had earned enough money —despite what was still to be collected or what was uncollectable, plus the very high number of refugees who didn't pay a cent and that the Cuban government pushed into the yacht— to liquidate the share of Papito's partners, to keep the boat for themselves and keep '*pan para mayo*' as Gretel said, remembering the old peasants sayings from her original land.

But there was another reason to stop those crazy trips at once.

Returning from the second trip Gretel sat Papito on the same steps of the old jetty from the beginning, she brought the beers this time, and, looking into his eyes, said to him:

"Papito, you just lost a crewman, your only crewman".

"Hey, don't be a wuss!"

"Do you know why I've been puking all the way home, comemierda?"

"Can't be!"

"Oh, no, not that you were sterile and I didn't have what it takes!" —She grabbed him, pretending to be furious, with two fingers on his chin—. "Don't you have two or three children out there, Mr. Papito?" —She laughed softly—. "There must even be five or six little chinese, if not more, your children in the Vietnamese Delta that you spend your life mentioning!"

For Gretel it didn't go unnoticed, and she felt a twist in her heart when she realized that Papito's eyes were wet.

"I should have realized, *coño*, I'm a beast, I've put you and the kid in dan..."

"Stop, stop, Papito, you didn't force me to do anything!" —She pulled affectionately, but firmly, one of his earlobes—. "Everything I do, and what I'll do with my life, I decide and will decide, always, is that clear, Papito?"

"You're very sick in the head, Gretel!" —She, smiling, wiped the tears rolling down his face with a napkin.

"Could be, could be, but you take it or leave it".

In fact, Papito and Gretel didn't work out as a stable couple.

They had never mentioned, or joked about the word love.

Gretel felt a tender affection for Papito, who recognized in his heart a beauty, inside and outside, that she had never encountered in another person, but she didn't want it with the fire with which her sister evidently had wanted Herman many years ago, or like she had wanted the stage girl herself. Of which, by the way, she knew that she had been picked up, along with the girl, by a sister she had never spoken about, and her freak husband was being held in Fort Chaffee, a prison and relocation center of the US federal government in the state of Arkansas.

Papito and Gretel made love from time to time, in a calm and pleasant way, like two wise friends who understood each other's needs: he kissed her, caressed her, licked her in the places she indicated without words and at the same time he said tender and not so tender things to her ear —she wasn't a saint— that excited her, while she herself masturbated to orgasm, and then allowed herself to be penetrated. And Gretel enjoyed it for the kindness and carefulness, until he achieved a full satisfaction, or she masturbated him while he told him, very lowly, depraved and foul things, *bárbaras*, as he called them, that could happen among women and who lit Papito until paroxysm.

"Papito, not only have I given you my virginity, *coño*, but now I'm going to give you a son too". She embraced him with a tenderness that made him weep again with emotion.

"You told me you weren't a virgin but a young lady". —He said with a sob.

"I don't remember that, Papito, you weren't dreaming?"

"Life is fucking beautiful, Gretel!"

He squeezed her tightly with both arms around her back and spoke in her ear:

"I know you love me a lot, but I also know you're not in love with me". —She couldn't see the two tears that ran down his cheeks, but felt them in her soul—. "I won't tell you that I care for you, that I love you like no one I've ever loved because I have a macho pride that forbids it, but I swear that while you want, I'm in this fucking land nothing more than for you, and for the boy or girl or whatever, and when you don't want I'll be there as well even if I have to shot you twice and throw you into the sea!"

"One is enough, Papito of my soul!" —she told him between little wails.

They cried like two brats who had just been hit, pressed against each other.

In March, with a nine-month huge belly, Gretel had, by a c-section, a pair of twins, a girl and a boy, who came to the world in perfect condition as Ana Donremí said to all who listened.

Everyone, Ana María, her children, Máximo, the Nica and her four kids, Ana Donremí and a desperate Papito to know the results, hug Gretel and have a beer, were sitting nervously in the waiting room of the Obstetric Surgery Department at Mercy Hospital, a health center belonging to the Catholic Archdiocese of Miami, a hospital that was characterized, among other things, by having a spectacular view of the bay, the port of Miami and the chain of islets of Key Biscayne, in addition to housing the Ermita de La Caridad, a small church raised with the tiny donations, coins and pesos, no more, of thousands and thousands of Cuban workers settled in Miami, dedicated to revere the more or less identical copy of the original image of the patroness of Cuba, the Virgen de la Caridad del Cobre.

Veneration that had spread outside Cuban territory, not only by the Miami Cubans but also for people of other nationalities, such as writer Ernest Hemingway, whose gold medal won along with the Nobel Prize for Literature rests in a glass urn in the back of the altar containing the original image in the sanctuary located in the village of Cobre, in the foothills of the Sierra Maestra, in the easternmost province of Cuba.

"Don't you think that they should marry?", Máximo told Ana María.

"Leave them as they are or as they decide, Máximo, Gretel always surprises by doing things better than all of us". —She threw her arm over her brother—. "She's almost thirty-six years old and it was time for her to have children, but from that to getting married..."

They walked very close together to the window from which the dazzling blue of the Atlantic Ocean was glimpsed between the keys and the mainland. "Gretel's Gretel, Máximo, and you know it as well as I do". —She gave an affectionate touch to her brother's shoulder—. "And she, my brother, will do what she decides, without anyone's help, *vaya*, whatever comes out of her... you know!"

"Yeah, she went to find someone unknown in Cuba and returned with a husband and a son, or two, in her belly, she's ridiculous, mi *hermana!*"

"And I think that, by the way, she has even become rich!"

They laughed like two kids.

A nurse beckoned them with her hand, a Cuban, of course, from the swinging doors of the entrance area to the operating rooms.

They're twins, a six-and-a-half-pound girl and a seven pounds boy!

"My God, how could she endure it for nine months?", Ana Donremí exclaimed, taking a silk handkerchief from the side pocket of her tailored dress.

"As everything in her life has been done, *mamá*, by being courageous!", Máximo said as he hugged her.

"And Papito? Where is Papito, then?", asked the Nicaraguan.

Papito was crying in a corner of the spacious room.

Ana María went up to him and lifted him up, hugging him.

"She's tougher than you from here to China, isn't she, Papito?" —she said very, very softly, as she pressed him to her breast to cry together.

"You don't know anything, Ana María, even if I told you!"

"Don't tell me anything, Papito!"

They were crying with sobs of joy.

"I know more than you can imagine, Papito!"

"I know!"

22

KEFLAVÍK NAVAL AIR STATION, 1989

The so-called Cold War was fought all over the planet, and some parts of the world: Indochina, Cuba, Central America, Berlin in the sixties and seventies, Angola, Congo, Lebanon, to name a few, became very hot, sometimes scorching.

We know all of this, but in other lesser known places, the North Pole and its adjacent waters are a good example, battles were fought, tests, rather, struggles and tests of force from enemy to enemy, face to face, which almost never were collected by the press, but also rubbed like a match to dynamite the real integrity of the globe, perhaps with greater danger for being unpredictable.

Keflavík, an almost unknown airbase to most inhabitants of Earth, located on the Reykjanes peninsula, fairly close —everything there is relatively close— to Reykjavik, the capital and largest city on the island of Iceland, *Islandia* to the latinos, a small volcanic archipelago tucked right between the tectonic plates of North America and Europe, which would give the Icelanders the pleasure of saying that they don't belong to either colossus, but they, more traditionalists, and following their history, prefer to feel European, when it suits them, of course.

From World War II to the last breaths of the Cold War, Keflavík, a few miles south of the Arctic Circle, was a prime meeting place for military aircraft, strategic atomic bombers included, of Soviets and Americans in the almost frozen waters of the North Atlantic.

Look at the map and you will see that between Iceland and the north coast of Russia there is only water, water with no owner, sometimes frozen, but not always.

It is scary, though not so much now, to see today the top-secret photos of the time of those flights of the North American Phantom F4-C driving away, with better or worse luck, the giant four-stroke

Tupolev 95, the 'Bears' according to NATO, loaded with atomic and hydrogen bombs, or, those of the Mig 21 and 23 stuck to the B-52 super-fortresses, with its eight jet engines, full of, of course, all of the above Armageddon artifacts.

A single mistake, a miscalculation, a moment of weakness, an ill-executed maneuver, a failure of some instrument aboard those devices, and the peace of the world would have gone to hell in a second.

But fate didn't want us to end our days as a planet, thank God, in a misjudgment or a wrong calculation of some of those young combat pilots of either side, which, of course, they were simple human beings, would have had bad days, hangovers, unhappy loves, family disputes and other stuff proper of the flesh, even if it is young and healthy.

And in Keflavík stood out, in the final days of the increasingly warm Cold War, as an officer specializing in modern vision radars over the horizon, young Lieutenant Herman Rubino Markis, «Rub», the eldest son of Ana María and the late Herman Markis.

As tourists, to spend a few hours with the boy on his weekend pass, and to also get to know that singular island, went, via New York and London, the ladies Ana and Gretel, two mature women free like the wind.

Gretel María, a brunette —she got her mother's hair and Latin beauty— passionate and vehement, pursued a master's degree in political science at Howard University, the old black community college in the capital, Washington, famous, apart from its teaching quality, in its relationship with the Kennedy's, Martin Luther King, Malcolm X, Desmond Tutu, Jimmy Carter and other leaders and advocates of civil rights. A place not very suitable for a white girl, according to the standards of those years, but ideal, for a good student from Yale, with excellent grades but with political ambitions not yet well defined, although towards the conscious search of that definition, and with many desires to know the deep strata of her country.

"No mom, I prefer to stay studying, you go alone and have a great time, you deserve it". —She hugged Ana—. "And be careful about what you do, eh!"

"We're two old ladies, Gretel María!"

"Fuck!" —The girl gave her the finger.

And Gretel's twins, who were almost eight years old, stayed in Miami with their grandmother, Ana Donremí, and the kind support of Máximo and her inseparable woman, because they shouldn't miss school and, besides, this was a trip, not everything was work and suffering in life, so that the two women went and travel the world and live it leisurely, with light baggage.

Ana María, who was still living in her pleasant and endearing Bethesda apartment. "I'm a routine and comfortable woman, haven't you yet noticed?", she said had had a couple of fleeting relationships in the last fifteen years.

She was going out, and sleeping with a doctor of Brazilian descent who was somewhat older than her, a good and very pleasant person, but definitely in search of a wife, a housewife who would bring his flip-flops and the house coat when he got home in the evenings.

One dawn, after a bustling and tiring night of sex dragging the increasingly pressing requests for marriage, and while she was taking a shower, it suddenly dawned on her that she enjoyed walking barefoot on her house, alone, free, prepare breakfast, exchange a few words with Suyin and dismiss their children for school, then get dressed and go, quietly to her work (where she met the doctor), so, she was tired of keeping this up, and ended it in an instant.

"Maybe I let a good marriage go, Gretel, but I didn't love him, and my apartment, which I will not change, is for me, for my children and Suyin, and for no one else".

Years later, with more than forty-five years, but as good looking as her mother in the old days, she met a thirty-two-year-old geneticist who was a graduate of the National Institute of Health, a Texan who moved her hormones around for a while. The boy, because he was a boy in appearance and way of thinking, at first showed a little clumsy tenderness, but very nice –she began to feel valued and satisfied– but in two months, when the boy got used to the company of the lady, the affair turned into a series of marathon sessions of long and strenuous sex. One morning Ana was surprised to realize, while she was putting on makeup to cover her dark eye circles in the mirror that the fucking boy was something like a perpetual motion machine that only subsided to give way to emotional and reticent talks about the incredible research that would lead him to win the Nobel Prize in the not-too-distant future.

And that was it.

"I stopped him flatly and advised him to find a girlfriend of his age. And you know what, mi *hermana*?" He followed my suggestion and he did".

"So soon?"

"Now the one with dark circles is the girl!"

"Are you jealous?"

"Relieved, Gretel, relieved!" —One could see the satisfaction in the calmness of their conversation. "No one like Herman, my little sister!"

Gretel laughed and made fun of her.

"The geneticist left you chafed down below, Ana, admit it!"

"You won't believe it, Gretel, he sucked my nipples so much, he didn't get tired, that fucking baby, that one night I proposed to prepare a couple of bottles of warm milk and meanwhile put some ice on my tits to relieve the swelling!"

"How awful!"

"Texan, Gretel, Texan. He the cowboy me the cow!"

Both of them were laughing out loud with those stories.

After the birth of the twins, Gretel devoted herself to them in body and soul, and Papito continued to be the good supplier as always, but one day he began to go out of control.

He bought a little house in the Roads, a small, quiet and very pretty neighborhood, like a cake wedge glued to the modernity of Brickell on its base and the two sides and the tip looking towards the center of Miami. A community that managed not to mingle too much with the exaggerated traffic and social tensions that had been uncovered after the Cuban exodus of the previous year. Well, Papito got the house under Gretel's name, only her, and he kept living on his own.

Gretel, too clever, realized immediately that the weeks when Papito wasn't there he was out at sea "earning his living" as he said.

The subject got dire when a cousin of his called her on the phone

one day to tell her that Papito was locked up in the County jail.

In half an hour Gretel was there, paid his bail —it wasn't very high because the accusations were not clear and apparently could only claim the illegal possession of an assault weapon, illegal at the time—, got a lawyer, paid with a check as an advance and signed everything necessary to get Papito out.

She, frowning like a furious animal, waited for him at the door of the detention center. When he, pale and annoyed was out, they both walked in silence to Gretel's car.

She opened the door and sat him on the passenger seat, turned around the car and got behind the wheel, started it and drove slowly, without saying a word, to a deserted place on the coast in the southern part of the city, below some neighborhoods of luxury mansions, Cocoplum (not Cocaplum, as jockers said), Gables States and a few others that were growing rapidly in those turbulent years of fortunes gained overnight.

She stopped the car in a little beach, facing the sea and turned off the engine.

She turned to him and looked at him straight to his face.

"Papito, if you want to become a billionaire for you, and only you, to enjoy it, that's your problem, this is a free country..."

"Look, Gretel, I..."

"Shut up and listen to me!" —He remembered, he couldn't help it, the red ax—. "If you want that, do it, but change your name and don't even come close to my life and that of my two children!" —She hit the wheel of the car with such force and anger that she almost broke her hand.

"But, and hear me well because I'm going to tell you once!" — She thrust the index finger of her right hand to his chest—. "If you keep looking for money the way you're doing it, and I don't care how you do it, but I can imagine". —She pressed her finger harder to his chest—. "I'm going to kill you like a mangy dog and I'm going to make you disappear, seriously, Papito, this time it's for real!"

"I..."

"Don't open your mouth, *cojones*!" —Papito felt something like fear, like that long, dreadful night in the Viet Cong infested Delta—.

If you keep doing this, you fucking idiot, you're going to stain the name and future of my children, and I'm not going to let it, I'm not going to allow it, you piece of shit!

Papito stepped back significantly.

"You made those children to me, Papito, because I opened my legs, and I don't regret it, and you can count yourself lucky that you are the only man, the first and the last, who put his dirty thing in my thing, but in the same way that I opened my legs once, because I wanted to, Papito, because I wanted to, I'll open your head and make you disappear, and I'm serious, Papito, very serious! "

Two seagulls flew past and squawked on the silent beach.

"For thirteen years I carried small bags of food and underwear for my brother in prison, you know this, and I would do the same for you, for a thousand years, a million years if need be, but not for such a low thing!"

"Gretel, I need to exp..."

"I don't want to hear it!" —She turned to look at the windshield of the car—. "Oh, and don't even think of showing with money at the house, not even a penny, absolutely nothing, I have the ovaries to earn a living decently, mine and my children's!"

She started the car with a deep, contained rage, she backed off with screeching wheels and got back on the road. She drove on the US-1 north bound near downtown and stopped on a corner.

"Get off, and if you're not willing to really work, change your life, please get out of our lives forever!"

When he got out, Gretel pulled the vehicle door toward her, to close it, with such force that the glass got knocked out of place.

"Your bail is paid and your lawyer is paid, now get out of my sight and fuck off!"

Papito sold the boat —or he sunk it very professionally in a cove on Isla Morada, south of Miami, to collect insurance as he confessed to her years later— and with that money and what he already had saved and had very well hidden, rented a concrete dock (with time he bought it) on the south bank of the Miami River, near its mouth in the bay, and began a business of repairing and remodeling of tourist ships, especially luxury yachts, which was turning, with hard work and efficiency, into a superb source of legal money, as he would tell his friends much later.

Gretel helped him with unscrupulous efforts and very wise advice, and he helped her with money, her salary, a generous salary, plus the twins cut, and dedication. More than that, devotion.

One day, while they ate, as they often did, at a seafood restaurant by the river, she told him:

"Papito, we can be proud, you and I, to have lived a nice and clean love story, I don't know if the biggest one in the world, but a good story, and if anyone doubts that, there are the twins to prove it".

She raised her glass of white wine and clinked his.

"But I think it's time, Papito, for you to get married, have a home like God intended, relax and stop having children all over the world".

"Gretel, I've just loved you, and you know it".

"Don't be childish, Papito, I know that you loved me very much and I, in my way, have loved you like nobody else in my life, but let's face it".

She took a long drink from her glass.

"If I had married you, you would have been bored, tired of me and my tediousness, my temper, my bossiness, my impertinence, and you'd be cheating on me all over town. In fact, you have a girlfriend, right now, here in Miami, or am I lying?"

"I... no, it's not..."

–Look Papito, I'm your best friend, the best in the world, and I won't let anyone take that from me, men or women, but marriage, sex... I'm going to be a little harsh. —She took another drink of wine and poured more into the glass to make time.

"What's happening with you is that all men think that they can 'save' lesbians with their love, with their caresses, and I'm a lesbian, homosexual, gay, whatever you want to call it, Papito, and I'm insurmountable... IN – SUR – MOUNT – ABLE, got it?" —She shook her head from side to side—. "And worst of all is that I like the way I am and I don't want to be saved, neither by you nor anyone, Papito, anyone!"

Gretel mussed Papito's hair.

"You saved me from a personal disaster, from insanity, you

straightened my life and gave me the best I've had in my life, that we have, the twins, and I saved your life, didn't I?" —She squeezed his strong hand—. Let's be what we have always been, you and me, since that dawn when I was going to kill you with an ax for kissing me on the back of my neck, remember? The best friends in the world.

After spending Friday and Saturday sightseeing with Rub, knowing the capital, having for breakfast fresh bread and Turkish coffee, having skyr as a snack, the yogurt of Icelanders, trying typical dishes, such as native lamb, slátur, some plain blood sausages according to Ana, a little fermented shark meat, the hákarl, and the marinated skin of a sheep's testicles, which made Gretel say:

"I don't like a man's balls, Ana, how am I supposed to like sheep's?" —which made Rub laugh out loud.

Coming in and out of the shops, buying local candies, making a visit to the church and the Hallgrímskirkja tower —what fucking difficult names these people had, shit!— and going around, in a car rented by Rub, a good stretch of the Hringvegur, the beautiful coastal road, much longer than they could imagine because, in fact, it circles the entire island. By those parts they visited the hot-water geysers, the hot-springs of the so-called Golden Circle, where people bathed buck naked "Oh, I like this, Gretel said", the half-frozen waterfalls —all with strange names that always ended in foss— where in one of them, Skogafoss, according to ancient Scandinavian legends, is buried, by the first Viking that came to these lands, a chest full of gold and when Gretel heard this, asked: what are we fucking waiting for? Let's start digging! The cliffs, the sharks' meat tanners where aunt and nephew formed a hilarious scene:

"My God, it smells like old man's piss!"

"Of course, Auntie, it's the urea that comes off the flesh because sharks don't have kidneys".

–Oh yeah? And how do they pee then? –And the three of them laughed non-stop.

They also saw, for the first time, blue ice which brought another joyful dialogue between them.

"Who entertains himself by painting the ice in that color?", asked Gretel.

"Don't be dumb, Aunt Gretel, the ice looks blue because it freezes at a high speed and it's very dense, so just the blue light rays goes through!"

"And everything you're explaining to us, you learn while you spy on the Bolsheviks, my son?" —She banged his head—. "And the dumb one is your mother, not me, let's be clear, ok?"

Ana María's belly ached because of laughter.

Tired and happy, they went back to the hotel to bathe and have dinner.

"Christian food please, or better, Cuban!", Begged Ana.

After a good conventional meal —international, as they called it—, tasty and well served, Ana María and Rub went back to the room to talk and drink Port, but Gretel, somewhat glum —that wasn't strange in her— decided to go and have a beer somewhere, alone.

Wrapped in a long beige leather coat with a matching scarf, she got into a bar, from which laughter and hotness seeped out, a few meters from the hotel. A group of girls were celebrating something, or just enjoying Saturday night in that barren, cold, half-empty land, where human warmth was much more necessary than in other places with warm weather.

Gretel sat down at the bar and ordered a glass of wine, but one of them, slender, kind, introduced herself as Johanna —the surname was unpronounceable, something like Sigurdartdottiring— approached her and asked her with great deference and education where was she from.

"I'm from Cuba, well, I'm actually Cuban-American".

"From the Caribbean!"

"I've been living in Miami since many years ago, you know?"

"But you have the sun, and life, inside, it shows!" —She grabbed her politely by the elbow.

"Are you waiting for someone?"

"No, I'm alone".

"Then come, come with us to enjoy the night, and tell us about your world, this icy island is very boring!"

They made a place for her and they gave her some taste of Brennivín, a strong potato drink with a cumin aroma, the national liquor of Iceland.

"Puff, how strong!"

"Do you know why the bottle has a black label?"

"No idea".

"Well, to frighten us and not drink it!"

They all laughed.

"But you drink it anyways?"

"But of course!" —They laughed like tinkling bells, or so it seemed to Gretel.

"And you know what the name means, Brennivín?"

"Not at all".

"Well, it means hot wine". —They poured some more into the small cup—. "Wait a while and you'll see how well you'll feel!"

"Believe me that I feel very, very good already!"

Gretel not only felt good because of the Brennivín, but also felt like family, as if she had lived there, in that warm piece of ice, for twenty years.

That night, even though the nights are incredibly short in the summer by those latitudes, for Gretel it flew by.

And of course, not in the hotel.

In heaven.

23

MIAMI, 1998

Gretel, wearing black Ray-Ban goggles and a baseball cap, so as not to be dazzled by the leaden sun of Havana on a cloudless summer day, drenched in sweat and feeling the salty drops run down her back into her jeans, in the groove between the buttocks. Thirsty and suffocating, she slips with damp fingers two twenty-dollar bills into the gray, dirty, baggy pocket of the gravedigger's work shirt, a mature man, wearing a frayed straw hat, wire-thin, with a four or five days hard beard, talkative and helpful. One of those Cubans made from hard work and not warming up their heads by thinking too much.

"My God, lady, this is my salary of four or five months, no, no, I can't accept it!"

Pride and necessity collided head-on.

"It's for your family, so that they buy something in my name and in the name of the deceased".

She puts her hand on the shoulder of the undertaker. "You don't know how much my family and I thank you for what you've done for us!"

"This is my job, ma'am, I spend all day with the dead".

"But you didn't have to do this today". —She points to the empty tomb, now she sees it small and abandoned, of which the man had already covered with earth and even with weeds and pebbles, so that no one notices that it has been removed.

"God bless you, ma'am!" —He kissed the two wrinkled, damp bills.

"If I had more, I would give you more". —Gretel feels her throat close as she says this lie, and for a moment she has the idea of opening the little purse that she carries around her waist and pull out five or six more bills, but she holds it.

"You can't even imagine what all of us, my wife and kids can buy with all the money you have given me!"

Gretel was looking at him and remembered what Papito said to her: "Don't give anyone too much money, Gretel, twenty or thirty dollars is a fortune in that country, don't forget, you can get in trouble". —He said when he was preparing her for the week-long trip to Cuba. Or they'll rob you if they think you're a millionaire, or the government notices and they may even detain you.

Gretel grabbed the rough cardboard box with the few remaining bones of her father, or those of someone who died like her father on the same day, and carefully stored it in a large white canvas bag with a royal palm painted and a red sign that said CUBALSE, a Cuban company of exclusive service to foreign tourists.

"Hey, ma'am, what a big hole at the back of the skull this dead man has, and forgive me the audacity to say such a thing, but..."

"There is nothing to forgive, it's the truth, but that is a very old story and it's no longer the case, so let's walk, you to yours and me to mine, we are both roasting under this sun, aren't we?"

Included in the box there were two bullets, flattened by the impact with the bones, which after many doubts and musings she throwed to the sea, one by one, as far as she could. She sits on the wall of the beautiful Malecón overlooking the Florida Strait and the Gulf Stream, while praying a quiet prayer and reaffirms that it's better to throw those two bullets that would almost certainly have been detected by the X-rays at the airport exit.

Then, she also pays an employee of a famous funeral parlor 'por la izquierda', where they keep vigil over the high officials of the Communist Party, the military with many stars, and the top intellectuals, if they were faithful to the poor and the party, of course, that died on the island, because they all die, we die, rather, in the end. Gretel payed the man to crush the bones and turn them into dust.

Powder that she'll put, once in the hotel room, inside a box of expensive Spanish talc, which she'll have to throw in the toilet little by little every day. She bought it at an exclusive foreign-exchange store, where she also bought soaps and perfumes at ten or twelve times the price that would have cost her in Miami, but what can you do, you have to pretend in the name of Rubino and Ana Donremí.

Gretel takes advantage of a week's stay for a few laps around Havana, a Havana that was her home, the space where she lived and suffered for twenty-eight years, where she thought she had found true love, once, a long time ago. But it is a Havana that has become alien, which she no longer recognizes as her own, one that turns its face and doesn't pay her any attention.

"Well, fuck you Havana!", She angrily said.

Then she took a noisy motorboat with plastic seats, as if she were a European vacationer in search of adventures and goes to pray to the Virgin of the Waters, a miraculous virgin who in turn is an African deity in the Regla church, a small fishing village on the other side of the bay, almost at the foot of the castle walls where her father was killed, her brother locked up and where Ana María met Herman.

"Such stories that fucking fortress has!" —She whispered looking at it.

A fortress from colonial times that is now a museum and an exotic recreation center for tourists eager to see unique things in history —what stories?— of the colonial Caribbean with its corsairs, slave ships, smugglers, coffers full of gold doubloons buried in solitary beaches and cutlass sword fights and duels with cannons between wooden galleons, rope and wind canopies, idiocy, nonsense for tourists, if only they knew what history is? But anyways, who cares about all that?

Finally, she leaves that Havana where she left her youth buried, a little piece of her heart —which reminds her of the silly lyrics of a very old song that sounded all the time on the radio and that now she can't remember— without looking back, turning her back as one does to a stranger that walks near.

She did what she went to do and when the plane took off, from the old airport of Rancho Boyeros to Miami, she understands, with relief, that her small and very personal police novel is going to have a good ending.

"Thank God!"

All of this Gretel is remembering while she's smiling, fulfilled and pleased, for one of the pictures of the high school graduation party of the twins, held in Rusty Pelican, a beautiful place just at the entrance, crossing the first bridge of the freeway to Key Biscayne. A place surrounded by sea and seagulls, of boats and sky. A party that

Papito proudly paid for, now an elegant potbellied gentleman with many gray hairs and sun spots on the forehead and the back of his hands, but still appealing to women, a little bit because of his macho appearance —if they had seen him in the 80's, damn!— and another bit by the bulging wallet he wears, smug, in the back pocket of the fine, custom-made English fabric trousers.

His wife, a Cuban beauty to rent balconies in her best times, but still very sexy, although, of course, with the help of some well-done aesthetic refinishing —which Papito payed— that erased her lines of expression, which the envious call wrinkles, and they repositioned her breasts, which they called boobs, to the right place where they were at the age of twenty.

"Gretel, I know you don't believe me, but I don't have erections, *vaya*, I don't get hard, if it's not with Cuban women with big tits like yours, *coño!*"

"You depraved, degenerate pig! Should I give you an ax blow to the very center of your head or should I tell your wife?" —She sees him blush and enjoys it, excited, by the lively and good memories that her rudeness brings—. "What's your choice, Papito?"

"The ax, Gretel, the fucking ax, that woman has an even worse bad temper than yours, and that's saying a lot!"

The woman, the wife of Papito, a daughter, more or less like Gretel, of a political prisoner that they released the year after the political earthquake of Mariel, fell in love with Papito in a dance, or a party, she doesn't remember well, in a Disco, and with work, with firm character and a lot of intelligence she has been herding him and enduring his things to a certain extent, for life's sake.

"*A cantazos*", as Puerto Ricans say.

She, Papito's wife, smart, intelligent, gets behind them and hugs them by the shoulders, putting her still very pretty face between the two.

"The twins in front, that this is their party, okay?" —The photographer shouts.

The Icelandic —she couldn't miss being in the photo— goes hip to hip with Gretel to make room for Ana María, aged, almost in her sixties, but dressed in the latest fashion and makeup like a queen, or even better. Few queens look like that this days.

"Johanna, girl, this isn't Iceland, push and make space for me, please!" —Ana María puts an arm around Johanna's back and pinches Gretel's ear.

"Annna!" —The Icelandic speaks with a slightly nasal, guttural accent, but speaks English very well, and even in Spanish. "I'm sticking my hip all I can, chiiica!"

"The hips, el caderón that the Finnish woman has!", Máximo says.

"Icelandic, Máximo, not Finnish", Gretel tells him.

"Isn't it the same?"

Máximo, the Nica, their four children and nine grandchildren, almost all of them babies, made the photographer —a famous musician of a line of famous musicians, his grandfather was named in Cuba 'The Wizard of the Keys'— who has learned to earn a living with the camera "you have no choice but to go were the money is, to despair".

"If you don't squeeze, you won't appear in the picture, are we clear or not?"

Ana Donremí is here no longer, at least not of present body, although her memory and her elegance floats in the environment. She died of a lymphoma six months before, but she left happy, knowing that she would rest next to her Rubino, little box against little box in the same drawer of the ossuary at the Calle Ocho Cemetery, at last!

And thanks to Gretel's mad trip, she brought the ashes of the deceased.

"God willing they are Rubino's!" —Gretel thinks but she doesn't say it. That doubt, in fact it doesn't have much importance, is only hers.

"This child, may God bless her, has given me the best gift I could ever receive, except, the wonderful gift of her children, my grandchildren". —Ana Donremí said as she wiped a tear, one, as it ran down her face.

Gretel, like always, when her mother was diagnosed with cancer and was given more or less a year to live, went to Máximo's house in Hialeah and from there they called Ana María, they explained the situation to her and she, Gretel, told the two that now she was going to

Cuba to find someone, not someone unknown but her father Rubino.

"Are you crazy, Gretel?", Máximo told her, now more worried about her than his mother.

"Yes, I am, but it's not foolishness, Máximo, I owe it to our mom, it's the least I can do in her last days".

"Then go where your heart tells you, Gretel!" —And looking at Máximo with a serious face, the nica snapped at him: Don't call your sister crazy, Máximo, she's the sanest and the bravest of the whole family, she reminds me of Doña Violeta, the one that stood against the Sandinistas.

Lieutenant Colonel Herman «Rub» Markis, decorated in the Gulf War of '91, pushes to get into the focus of the camera, and he isn't alone, he pulls his sister Gretel María, now a beautiful state representative for Maryland, the state that she made her own but without forgetting her Asian, Latino and Cuban roots.

In the front, the jokester Papito, there is always a comedian in big families, grabbed Suyin, turned into a little raisin, maybe eighty or ninety pounds, no one knows her age, even herself, and lifts her with his hands around the waist for her to be seen in the photo.

"That's how I like to grab women!"

"Suyin is too much of woman for you, Papito!", said Ana María, dying from laughter.

"I know something of Chinese women that you don't know, okay?"

"I not Chinese, young man!", Suyin almost shouts while moving her tiny legs in the air.

"Young maaaan!"

A choir rises from the group, making everyone look to the front, smiling, and the photographer takes advantage of the instant that has been given to him, unwittingly, by that skinny little china woman like a little twig, to shoot the shutter of his Roleiflex.

"Papito, young maaan!"

"Here, here, look at the birdy —the photographer raises his arm and snapping his fingers".

"Click".

24

THA YAI, 2006

Suyin died peacefully, without tension or pain, at the end of May.
From the moment, a couple of years ago, when doctors diagnosed her a chronic degenerative, but eventually mortal disease, Ana María tried to convince her to travel to her land accompanied by her, to say goodbye to her family.

But the Thai begged her to spare her from such a journey, and she vehemently expressed the firm will to die with them who had been, so she said, her true family and where she had had her only true home for the last forty years.

"When my soul go, you make with my body what you want, Ana, but let me leave from here, that is my desire!"

"And your ashes, Suyin?"

The Indochinese are not given much to ambiguity or circumlocution when it's something as natural and predictable as death.

"If you want send there or leave here, it does not matter!"

Concluding the cremation ceremony of Suyin's body, Ana María gently and lovingly collected the rosewood urn with the ashes of the Thai woman, went to her apartment to rest —she had spent the last week with her at the hospital— and to devise a plan that had been going on in her head for several days.

Now the ark, the small wooden urn with the few ashes of what was Suyin's body, rested on top of the drawer, beside the red wine case with the gold medal —which had finally been given to her and her sons at a ceremony at the Pentagon after September 11, 2001— that had been posthumously won by the hero Herman Markis, and that Ana had seen, alone, fleetingly, thirty years earlier.

Lying in bed, in pajamas, after a relaxing bath of warm water and aromatic salts, taking a delicious and stimulating Japanese matcha tea, which gently filled the whole room with sandalwood, Ana María grabbed her BlackBerry, read the first messages and immediately made a call to Miami.

"Gretel, mi *hermana*, do you dare to follow me on an adventure?"

"Are you going to rescue someone in Cuba, Ana?"

"No, mi *hermana*, those trips to the island were made for you alone, what I want to do is bring Suyin's ashes to her land, to her house, or rather, to the home of her ancestors!"

The cry of a newborn was clearly heard on the other side of the phone.

"Count with me right now, sis!"

Gretel was giving the feeding bottle to the little offspring of her daughter-in-law and her son Mario Antonio.

"Do we include Mariel and the woman that came from the ice in the adventure?"

"Of course, Gretel, it would be great if they came with us!"

"Deal, Ana, I'll talk to them right now".

With Gretel María, who had long been married and already had two children, she knew she could count on, for she had also been in the last moments of Suyin and had talked, walking the lengthy corridors of the large Walter Reed hospital, about Ana's decision.

"If you can postpone the trip for two or three weeks, mami, I'll leave my things in order at the Capitol and I'll join you".

Gretel María had obtained the previous year a seat at the state of Maryland in the National House of Representatives, the Congress, and according to many analysts (especially the ones that communicated with her party) she was doing a very nice job.

The five women —six in fact, because in the rosewood casket, almost in all probability, was Suyin's benevolent *phi*—, a whole female troupe, met in Washington —Gretel and Mariel flew in from Miami and Johanna from Iceland via London— and departing from Dulles Airport, they traveled first to San Francisco, already on the Pacific Ocean, where they took a three-day vacation.

"Suyin is enjoying seeing us enjoy life!", Gretel María said with a fresh smile.

"No, not only she's seeing us but is here with us, or don't you feel her presence?", Mariel replied, shuddering.

Mariel, Mario Antonio's twin, was making a career as a concert pianist —she studied eight and ten hours a day when other girls her age played house and watched the cartoons on TV— who was on her way of becoming a star of international scenarios before the age of thirty.

With a strong classic music background acquired at the sophisticated and expensive Berklee College of Music in Boston —which was happily paid by Papito and Gretel when they became convinced that music was really her thing and not law or business— the girl, guided by the wise advice of innovative pianist Joanne Brackeen, one of her favorite teachers at Berklee, began to move towards jazz, studying teachers such as Art Tatum, Lennie Tristano, Oscar Peterson, Bill Evans, Herbie Hancock and the great Thelonius Monk, until finding through the longest way and with hard work her Latin and Afro-Latin roots in the rhythm and incredible phrasing of Hilton Ruiz, Bebo Valdés and his son Chucho, Eddie Palmieri, Emiliano Salvador, Peruchín and Michel Camilo.

"Damn, and I just grew up hearing Elvis, The Beatles and Benny Moré", Grumbled Papito but swollen inside with pride.

Then, always searching, researching, digging and, of course, finding, she was introduced, with the alert and tuned ear to a superlative level of excellence, on the piano rock of the murdered John Lennon, and thence to Elton John, Tori Amos and Billy Joel, recurving then, in an impressive jump that only a person with a mastery and constancy out of this world could realize, towards the study, and the divulgation, of feminine pianist values, past and present. Values such as those of Argentina's Martha Argerich, María Joao Pires of Portugal, María Teresa Carreño of Venezuela, the English Myra Hess, Helene Grimaud of France, the Mexican-Cuban Margot Rojas, Clara Haskil of Romania, Brazilian Guiomar Novaes, the Cuban women Cecilia Arizti, María Cervantes and Zenaida Manfugás —with whom she shared in New York pleasant and informative talks on more than one occasion— and the extraordinary Spanish concert-master Alicia de Larrocha.

She came from playing, as a young guest artist in New York and Philadelphia, respectively, with the Chinese portents Yundi Li and

Lang Lang and from recording a song, in a Miami Beach studio, accompanying the invisible Isis.

The Jumbo 747-400 from Delta Air Lines arrived at the new — they had just opened it to the public— and spectacular Suvarnabhumi Bangkok airport in mid-afternoon, it was slightly raining but the sun was visible in some holes in the clouds, and after going through Customs and picking up their luggage, two carts filled to the top, they met at the passenger's exit with the eldest son of Dr. Sirikit, a man of considerable age, a physician just like her, and the only one of her three children who had settled in the country.

"How's your mother, *muchacho*?" —She hugged him affectionately and he embraced her.

"She's been ninety years old since the day before yesterday and is still giving us orders, cooks and fights for the poor quality of the food we bought for her, ma'am!"

"A genius and a figure up until...!", Ana didn't finish the aphorism.

The man had brought his Suburban van to drive all those women and their luggage: suitcases, briefcases, backpacks, dressing cases and 'little feminine shit' according to Gretel, to the hotel.

"This looks like a Marine's landing!", Gretel María said.

"Worse, my child, it's a plague of Cuban women!", Gretel replied.

After several days touring the capital, its pagodas, the temple of Wat Arun, its buddhas, the royal palace, known as the Grand Palace, markets, sailing in express boats by the Chao Phraya, the canals and its housing boats or their market barges, excellent haute couture shops, glimpsing from afar the red-light districts which begged Gretel to ask:

"Why don't you let me explore those places by myself?", Johanna replied to her with all the sweetness she was capable of speaking in English:

"Becauuuse you will disappear in them forever, Gretel!"

Expensive restaurants and street food stalls, sometimes much tastier and infinitely cheaper, dealing with thousands and thousands of street vendors, the gigantic traffic (they loved the BTS air train), the roadblocks and the incessant crowds.

"It's like Manhattan, but speeding at all stops!", Mariel pointed out.

160

Climbing the lofty viewing point of Baiyoke Tower #2, Bangkok's tallest building, and strolling among the lindens and oaks of Lumphini Park which impressed Ana María:

"It looks like a little paradise in hell! In my time here this park didn't exist!", Exclaimed Ana María.

And even visiting the American School, now much larger and more modern, where Ana didn't find anyone she knew —although she and her group was received very kindly— but, to her surprise, she ran into herself, full bodied, smiling, accompanied by other teachers and employees, wearing low shoes, socks and wearing a white school-style blouse and miniskirt, in the gallery of historical photographs attached to the main hall.

"My God, how could I dress that way! —She shook her head, incredulous, from side to side—. That woman doesn't look like me!

"Wow, Mom, what a provocative outfit!" —Gretel María made a sassy grin with her lips—. "They were very modern here forty years ago!"

"Forty years, it can't be, my God!"

"You're right, Ana, in the photo says 1965, so only forty-one!", Gretel told her with her characteristic irony.

"Fuck you, Gretel, that's not funny!"

They set off for Tha Yai at dawn, descending south from Bangkok, along Highway 402, which runs down the entire Malaysian peninsula (both countries share this relatively narrow strip of land from the west, the Gulf of Thailand and across the Andaman Sea) until entering, by a bridge, the island of Phuket.

Suyin and her entire family had lived for generations in the vicinity of Tha Yai, a small village that had grown to now be a village of some importance, and is the last on dry land just before the entrance to Phuket.

When the tin mines were depleted in the 19th century, leaving thousands of inhabitants of the area without economic support, Tha Yai men began to earn a living with rubber. Rice, in that area, was always for their own consumption and harvested, and still harvested, by women, but the tourist boom on the island of Phuket and its incredible beaches, which became fashionable in the West during the

Indochina War, gradually displaced the cultivation and bleeding of the hevea (Rubber Tree) and have been attracting almost all the available labor in its surroundings. And from that, from tourism, now live the relatives of Suyin and all their neighbors.

After the questioning, the usual greetings and courtesies to welcome such important visitors, the ashes of the Thai woman were placed with extreme respect in the house dedicated to the spirits, a small structure made of cement and wood with a sort of gabled roof house set above it. In front of this simple construction is a tiny esplanade in which low tables are placed and on them, covered with carpets, candles are lit, fruits and other foods and colored fabrics are placed with invocations to the beneficial spirits of the ancestors.

After the small family ceremony ended, to which Ana and all her companions were especially invited, a simple meal was prepared and toasts were made for the event.

"This is how I would like to be sent to the other side, Ana, with a good drinking!" —whispered Gretel into Ana's ear without losing her composure.

The group of women, after a loving and grateful farewell for which the whole Suyin family was present, continued on their way across the bridge to the island and went to one of the modern Phuket hotels. There, after enjoying the beach and rest, and the superb massages, for four days, they returned the van they had rented in the capital and went back by plane to Bangkok, from the small but busy Phuket airport, to continue their way back to the United States.

"Suyin has returned with her ancestors, mom, but we'll have her memory". —Gretel María remarked with a hint of sadness.

"Something more than her memory, Gretel". —Ana María dropped in a pose of mystery.

"I don't understand".

"Half of her ashes remain in my house".

"Really, mom?"

"Of course, Gretel María, her generous *phi* may be able to cross the seas, but it seemed fair to me that some remained with us, just in case!"

The whole women's platoon sighed with relief at the same time.

25

WASHINGTON D.C. 2021

Andover House, the classic and elegant building where Gretel María Markis has her apartment —her married name and everyone knows this, is Steinbeck— the newly announced secretary of state of the new United States government, is three blocks from the Logan Circle and one from the Thomas Circle Park, in the very center of the city of Washington, the nation's capital.

Looking to the left from the glazed balcony of the cozy apartment you can see, almost within reach, the glistening white dome of the Capitol, and to the front, perhaps a little bit to the right, among the groves, the White House ceiling and beyond the roundabout, the fine, tall needle of the Washington Monument, blazing, illuminated by powerful bulbs that shine from below with the red, blue, and white colors of the North American flag.

A block and a half from the White House, this one is directly to the front, is the old, though recently renovated Hotel Willard. An old class Hotel, where in one of its emblematic halls, back in distant 1861, was held the first and last meeting between the emissaries of the southern rebels and some important officials of the northern government, the Federal Government, which could have avoided the Civil War, but fate, or pride, arrogance and the blind reticence of men was interposed and the bleeding to come became reality.

Farther to the right, half-hidden by the huge blocks of concrete and stonework that have been growing over the years in Foggy Bottom, the old brewery neighborhood adjoining the river, now a source of American power and money, the golden glow of the white marble can be seen, blazing by the intense illumination, of the monument to Abraham Lincoln. And behind, the river, the Potomac, a wide and dark tape in which boats were loaded with visitors, tourists, music, food, drinks and colored lights.

Although with much work ahead, the President's inauguration will be on January 20th and hers the next day —less than fifteen days away—, Gretel María made time that cold winter night at the capital to meet with her relatives. And while she, her husband, a former retired astronaut, and her three children, men and women now, deliver drinks and canapés, no waiters or people from outside, just family, Aunt Gretel, straight and elegant, tall and slender as always, sophisticated, haughty, with seventy-five years on her back but that made her seem like sixty, retires in silence towards a corner of the glazed terrace, with a half-filled broad glass of cold white wine, a California Chardonnay aged in oak, somewhat acid, expensive, as she likes to savor them.

She leaves the bustling and joyful group alone, in her calm pondering, taciturn, very much in her style, and it's a family tradition to respect it.

While savoring the wine, sip by sip, seated in a rocking brown leather chair, lustrous and fluffy, warm, looks indolently through the superb landscape that is offered to her to the enjoyment of her eyes on that night of celebration and jubilation.

"Who was going to tell me that I would live like this thirty years ago, damn!", She mumbles to herself.

And then she reviews the troops, very slowly, as in a film that is projected frame by frame, of her life. A life a little long —she smiles mockingly—, and also reviews those who are here, and those who aren't.

Widowed three times, a cheerful widow, she laughs again with malice, with the slyness of a mischievous little girl, though she never got really married, or went through notaries, signing of papers, witnesses and all such nonsense, "May God our Lord not allow it!" she thought.

Widow of the stage girl —what happened to her?—, time killed her, the forced separation, the necessity of the moment, the misery, the lie, the distance, the fear of the future, the discouragement; Widow of Papito, a man, a complete man, who truly loved her like the mad wise man that he was, and that she also loved, in her own way, the father of her children, the grandfather of her grandchildren. A heart attack killed him in his seventies, and he died well, without pain, without a complaint, quick, content, rich, living at his leisure, on the run. And also, a widow of Johanna, her Icelandic, the white female, soft as fresh snow, with red hairs and a hungry mouth with which she always dreamed, unknowingly; she was killed by a stupid road accident when she had reached the pinnacle of her political career in the parliament of her ice island and her constant and faithful love.

Gretel makes a rascal grimace, fun, like the rascal that she is, learned in love, knower and teacher of the existence, already an owner of experience.

"It wasn't a bad life, it was hard and laborious sometimes, but good, honest!", She keeps thinking.

Ana María, her soul sister, left three years ago. She fell ill for some time, but until the last minute she remained lucid and cheerful, worried about people, always ready to help, sincere, and not being with her daughter today, in such a beautiful and special moment, hurts Gretel, and that pain tightens her chest.

She sheds a single tear, and wipes it with the back of her left hand. She raises her glass of good wine and offers a toast for her:

"May you, my little sister, and crazy Herman see this moment, from the sky, or from anywhere, but together, *coño*, together forever!", She sighs.

Máximo is still on this earth, but his brain is gone. The death of the nica was too much for him. Heaps of children, grandchildren and great-grandchildren surround him. Already she lost count of how many there are, but it reassures her that they have turned out good, if not all, a good part of them, and that's enough and it makes her happy.

He was always a good guy, faithful, kind, simple, and as he proved in prison, heroic in his own way.

"A toast to you, Máximo, and may your nica come get you soon, so that you may be with her!" —She says and takes a sip of the excellent wine to the health of Máximo's soul, not his body, that body is no longer worth anything and living is not that.

"Well!" —She smiles once more and also toasts for her—. "To

your health, nica, and hurry up, Máximo is waiting for you!"

Her daughter Mariel and her son Mario Antonio turn 40 this year.

"Jesus, will these guys finally make me feel old?"

The three-star general, in civilian clothing, Herman Rub, carefully opens the glass door, reaches for Gretel a bowl of anchovies and Spanish olives, preferring that to the caviar, which she takes with indifference and thanks him with affection, he carefully turns back to close the door.

"How far will this brat go?", she thinks, and laughs, for he is almost sixty, no, fifty-five, more or less.

Lost in thought again, remembering things that in hindsight sometimes seemed impossible but when they happened you had to pay for them.

Mario Antonio, her son, the son of Papito, appears and tells her:

"Mom, does it bother you if I leave the door slightly ajar so you can hear Mariel?"

"No son, on the contrary".

That son, her son, will be named, immediately after the inauguration of the new government, ambassador in Cuba. He's young, has a beautiful wife and three children, her grandchildren, knows the world, politics, speaks Spanish perfectly, and his roots, because she, Papito, his four grandparents, are, were, from there, and he's happy and anxious to get to know that island, its people, the land of his origins.

"God help him!" —And Gretel raises the cup to the sky, for him.

And she silently invokes the same prayer to the virgin of the waters that once, more than twenty years ago, she prayed, with faith, to implore courage and encouragement to illegally remove from the rough land of the cemetery of Havana the remains of her Father and bring them back to the hands of Ana Donremí. The same prayer that gave her the strength to throw those two bullets into the water, those two ties to a past that was due, it was time to leave it behind.

"And may the virgin of the waters guide him to do good, Amen!"

Mariel, her daughter, is playing, with the softness of her hands and the temperamental force she expresses on every occasion, like the great artist she is, —As Time Goes By—. Recreates that old and beautiful piece, that theme that tells so much to her, in the glazed black lacquered piano, glittering on the side of the large living room.

Gretel interrupts her thoughts and listens to the melody, excited, slight, as suspended in the clean air of a high mountain. A feeling of euphoria, of trust surrounds her, expanding and suspending, briefly, the passage of time.

It is not old music, it is simply music, melody, it is like life, it goes on and on like sand between the fingers without ever stopping, no matter what we do to stop it, change it or convert it to our absurd designs.

She stands, agile, like the girl she's always been, a girl with a somewhat sullen face and heart of gold, healthy, open, who has always carried, in the storms and the calm, in the good, the bad and the worst, in the center of her chest.

Lying, lying to herself is easy, but it's not and has never been her thing. Always seeking the truth is difficult and she's not convinced that it's worth trying. Is it not better to leave —she thinks— each to its own, free, without the obstacles and the brakes that prejudices and fears impose on people?

If you don't know yourself well, why seek ungrateful truths in people? Why one has to know so many useless things of the past that already happened and that it doesn't return?

"Why ask so much about them?", She is surprised saying it.

She stands deftly and walks slowly, with her glass of wine almost empty in her hand, crosses the glass door and enters the warm room moving like a queen. She approaches the piano, puts the cup on top, pushes it to the side with an elegant gesture, and leans on it.

She smiles at Mariel, her daughter, who now plays only for her.

And Mariel smiles at her.

Radiant and beautiful.

INDEX

Havana, 1959..11

Havana, 1962..15

Guanabo Beach, 1963 21

Key West, 1963.....................................27

Miami, 1963 31

Bangkok, 1965 37

Tapao Air Base, 1965...........................43

Royal Thai Air Force Hospital, 1965.............51

Long Tieng Base, 1967.........................57

Lima Site 85, 1968 63

Honolulu, 1968 69

Bangkok, 1972 75

Don Muang Airport, 1973 81

Chiang Mai, 1973 87

Mekong River, 1973 93

Langley, Virginia, 1974........................99

Bethesda, Maryland, 1979.................................107

La Habana, 1980 115

 Puerto de El Mariel, 1980..................................121

Key West, 1980..129

Miami, 1981 135

Keflavík Naval Air Station, 1989 141

Miami, 1998 151

Tha Yai, 2006...157

Washington D.C. 2021 163

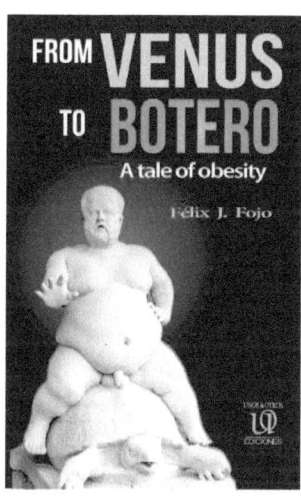

Félix J. Fojo

BORN
....
La Habana, Cuba

LIVES
....
Puerto Rico

He is a doctor, a
scientific promoter
and lover of the
history. Exprofesor
of the chair of
surgery of the
university of
havana. He is editor
of the medical
Magazine of Puerto
Rico "*Galenus*".